Lucy Cecil White Lillie

Prudence

a story of æsthetic London

Lucy Cecil White Lillie

Prudence
a story of æsthetic London

ISBN/EAN: 9783337311582

Printed in Europe, USA, Canada, Australia, Japan

Cover: Foto ©Andreas Hilbeck / pixelio.de

More available books at **www.hansebooks.com**

PRUDENCE.

"THERE WAS A CERTAIN SPLENDOR IN HER EYES."

[PAGE 15.

PRUDENCE

A STORY OF ÆSTHETIC LONDON

BY

LUCY C. LILLIE

ILLUSTRATED BY GEORGE DU MAURIER

NEW YORK

HARPER & BROTHERS, FRANKLIN SQUARE

1882

ILLUSTRATIONS.

PRUDENCE.

I.

THE first time Prudence Marlitt appeared in English society was at a dance at the Jamison-Poynsetts'. Mrs. Poynsett, as every one knows, is the wife of the famous R.A., and is herself a leader of æsthetic fashion in that region hovering between Kensington and Belgravia, and known as " Passionate Brompton." The highest forms of art, culture, and even science are expressed within the Poynsetts' hospitable walls; all the impressive social influences of the day gather new force when diffused by Mrs. Poynsett or her daughters; young poets can put their emotional impressions into verse when gazing upon the dado of Mrs. Poynsett's inner drawing-room; artists can gather that inspiration needed for their work by studying the willowy angles and sadly sunken eyes of the elder Miss Poynsett; yet there is nothing oppressive in the suggestions of the beautiful house — in the courtesy and grace of its occupants. They are "æsthetes," and they look forward to something even more æsthetic in the future, but the young ladies are very young, and still human enough to enjoy a dance; so that once or twice in the season cards are issued for an evening which will include some hours devoted to Terpsichore. But, at the same time, Mrs. Poynsett's friends well know what is required of them, even on such an occasion, in the way of costume. The *feelings* as well as the tastes of the company must be consulted; for are we not so delicately organized to-day that we must be saved any kind of artistic shock? As Barley Simmonson, a constant visitor at the Poynsetts', remarked, " There is power to *pain*—actually to pain—in that shade of our youth known as magenta or solferino, just as there is the power to lull anguish into calm "—and here Mr. Simmonson smiled with ineffable tenderness—" in Bordone's reds."

On the evening in question two American ladies made their way rather late toward the room where Mrs. Poynsett was receiving her guests. They approached with that air which comes less of beauty and grace than of social distinction. They were both young, and handsome as American women are expected to be abroad, but the younger and unmarried sister had the charm of a peculiar piquant intellectuality. It was difficult to say wherein this was expressed. She had delicate, dark eyebrows, rather inclined to be supercilious;

MRS. BOYCE AND MISS ARMORY.

eyes and lips ready enough to be merry, yet full of
thought; a nose and chin that were nearly fault-
less; and a profusion of the softest brown hair
coiled *à la Grecque* low upon her neck. She was
bright and lovely, and I am sure she knew pre-
cisely how valuable such adjuncts to a young
lady's appearance in society are, yet there was not
a touch of arrogance in her manner. She wore her
costume of pale yellow brocade, with its flutterings
of old lace and quaintly wrought silver ornaments,
as easily as she would have worn her riding-habit
in the Row; yet something half amused at her
own way of contributing to the artistic effect of
the company was evident in the pose of her charming head, in the smile which curved her pretty
mouth. The elder lady, whose good looks were
of the reddish-blonde type so favored to-day, was
dressed, with great effect, in a gown the cut and
color of which reminded one strongly of Titian's
women. She was an ardent disciple of the new
gospel of the "æsthetes," and felt herself one of a
chosen few, but she moved with the languorous
grace necessary when one has yards of plush and
satin to consider, and seemed to have no idea or
desire of creating a sensation. The dark and the
blonde beauty, however, were peculiarly charming as they came up the crowded corridor, and
the names, "Mrs. Boyce and Miss Armory," duly
announced, caused a certain degree of interest

among the people gathered about the first door-
way.

"At last!" said Mrs. Poynsett, holding out a
friendly, tired hand. "Now, my dear, where is
your wicked husband?"

"Oh," said Mrs. Boyce, with her pretty smile,
"he was *so* sorry! But at the last moment an
American friend turned up, and he could not
possibly leave."

"And are you ready to dance, Helena?" said
the hostess, looking at Miss Armory with fond admiration. "You American girls are always in demand. There is young Benison looking at you,
and I know what that means."

"Of course I am ready to dance," said Helena
Armory, "and Dick Benison is a capital partner;
but, dear Mrs. Poynsett, can't we stay here a moment to look on? It is all so beautiful!"

A dance necessarily makes decoration out of
place, but in this first room enough of color remained to give an Oriental splendor to the scene.
Heavy and pompous as were the fabrics, the wax-
lights and the languid fragrances filling the room
softened the effect, making it almost like some bit
of dream-land. Against the rich and somewhat fan-
ciful background the artistic figures were most effective. In the distance the dancers were whirling
to the strains of the "Sweethearts" waltz. Nearer
to the archway in which Miss Armory and her sis-

ter were standing were various suggestive groups:
pretty girls in quaint gowns; dowagers splendid in
diamonds and æsthetic colors; one or two fashion-
able beauties reviving the last century in their
attire and their frivolous animation; people with
nothing to do or to say trying to extract intensity
from the brilliancy of their surroundings. Miss
Armory was used to such companies, and knew
what to expect, yet she enjoyed looking about
her with good-humored criticism before she responded to the appeals of young Mr. Benison.

It was in this first careless survey of the room
that Prudence Marlitt came in view — a girl of
twenty one or two, dazzlingly pretty, sitting against
a gorgeous screen, which made a background whose
brilliancy seemed only to enforce her own. She
was gazing eagerly at her companion, Barley Simmonson himself, and her uplifted face shone beneath the radiance of candle-light with charming
effect. There was a certain splendor in her eyes,
a Southern tint in complexion that made her red-
dish-brown hair peculiar; but Miss Armory's memory, stored with all that was precious in Continental
art, failed her as she tried to think of anything so
lovely as this girl sitting in a shabby white muslin
gown against the splendid screen. She was talking to Simmonson with an air that was simply
adorable; there came a dimple in her cheek as she
smiled, showing her pretty teeth; a childlike ra-

diance was about her mouth and eyes; but it was difficult, thought Miss Armory, to decide whether the girl were thoroughly versed in the arts of coquetry, or a Miranda, "untravelled and unseen."

"Oh, I see whom you are looking at," exclaimed Mrs. Poynsett. "That is an American girl—a Miss Marlitt. I think she is the loveliest creature on earth. But was there ever such a gown!"

"Lovely! She is perfect," said Mrs. Boyce. "An American? Helena, we knew some Marlitts once."

"I am really quite bothered about her," said Mrs. Poynsett, sinking her voice. "All the men in the room are talking about her; yet, do you know, she has come entirely alone! *Quite* unchaperoned! I suppose it might do in America, but it certainly looks odd in London."

"Dear Mrs. Poynsett," exclaimed Mrs. Boyce, opening her gray eyes widely, "it would *not* do in America. There must be some mistake; and she looks such a perfect lady! Did you invite a chaperon?"

"Of course. She has just come to London with her aunt, a Mrs. Crane. They brought a letter to me from Colonel Wheeler; but all this divine young thing did when she appeared this evening was to apologize for her aunt's being obliged to stay at home. A cold or something! In a minute more I had to introduce half a dozen men to her. Barley Simmonson, as you see, is tremendously taken with her, but he'll tell every man at the 'Arts' about it to-morrow.—My dear Helena, how lovely your yellow gown is! Quite as good as Ellen Terry's.—How do you do, Mrs. Jenness?"

And Mrs. Poynsett's kindly hand began again to be engrossed. Mrs. Boyce and her sister remained silent a moment, watching Prudence with deep admiration. Mrs. Boyce is a most decided person. To watch her languid movements, her slow smile, her sleepy gray eyes, you would never think her capable of any impulsive action, but at heart she is one of the most impetuous women I know. When Mrs. Poynsett had finished speaking, there was a peculiar glow upon Mrs. Boyce's face.

"Helena," she said to her sister, "wait here a moment. I think I can arrange it with that poor child."

And so saying, she deliberately crossed the room to the peacock screen, where she smiled pleasantly upon Prudence and Lord Bairham's heir.

Barley Simmonson was conducting the conversation; but Miss Marlitt was listening, with her charming smile and little words now and then of assent, wonder, dissent perhaps, or interrogation. Into the conversation Mrs. Boyce came with a graceful sweep of her draperies which attracted Simmonson's attention.

"My dear," she said, in her soft voice, laying one hand upon Miss Marlitt's shabby sleeve, "I don't

think I can let you dance much more to-night;"
and with that the accomplished hypocrite beamed
upon the young man. "Don't persist, Mr. Simmonson; I can't let Miss Marlitt tire herself, or
her aunt will think me a very poor chaperon."

And before any one of the three had time to
think about it, Barley Simmonson had bowed and
moved away. Prudence had made room for her
impromptu chaperon upon the crimson bench, and
was looking at her with a wondering, lovely gaze.
Mrs. Boyce was perfectly undisturbed.

II.

"My dear," said Mrs. Boyce, "you must excuse me for what I have done; I thought you would be glad afterward. You see, in London a girl is criticised for coming to an evening party alone, and—I am an American myself—I know how English people can talk of us sometimes. Do you understand me?" and Alice Boyce looked at the girl with gentle friendliness.

. Little Miss Marlitt flashed one of her sweet looks upon her new friend. There was humility, gratitude, comprehension, in her glance.

"Oh, of *course*, I understand!" she exclaimed, quickly, putting one of her hands into Mrs. Boyce's. "How good of you!" The color swept across the girl's cheeks; her voice trembled. "How thoughtful! Oh, thank you! Yes, yes, I know. My aunt could not come, but she said it would be too bad to disappoint me; and Jonas Fielding, a friend of ours, brought me to the door, and will call for me at one o'clock. Have I done anything *very* dreadful?" she added, wistfully, and cast a nervous glance in the direction of Mrs. Poynsett's magnificent shoulders.

At this Mrs. Boyce grew very encouraging. She tried to set the girl completely at ease, and there was a charm in her manner which Prudence, in spite of her bewilderment, felt at once. She looked at the pretty, splendidly dressed young woman with soft gratitude.

"I am Mrs. Boyce," said that lady, "and you must consider me your chaperon for the evening. Now will you tell me all about yourself, dear? I shall see that your partners are not all frightened away."

Prudence gave Mrs. Boyce's hand another pressure. "There is not much to tell," she said, simply; and she told her meagre little history with an air of charming frankness. To begin with, she said they came from Ponkamak, in Maine; she was an orphan, educated by Jonas Fielding's father, and lately she had lived with her aunt, Mrs. Crane; she had been at school in Boston for a year; she had taught school herself for three or four months. Although these seemed but the dullest outlines, there really was little shading to put in. Prudence Marlitt, up to the present hour, had certainly led the colorless existence which with so many American women in the country grows grayer and grayer as years go by. She talked of herself with absolute simplicity, yet with an air that showed her practical common-sense. Mrs. Boyce understood her perfectly: she had thought out life, but had never lived; she had read and studied hard, no doubt, with no opportunity for exchanging an idea; and now she was unquestionably the most charming object in one of the most renowned drawing-rooms of London. The suggestiveness of it all was to Mrs. Boyce peculiarly striking.

"My aunt is very much interested in women's rights," Miss Marlitt continued, seeing that her listener's interest grew, "and also in the international copyright. She has corresponded with a great many distinguished people about it. It is so nice to have their autographs. We are hoping to see Carlyle."

"That will be very nice," assented Mrs. Boyce. And then she added: "I see my young friend Mr. Benison is looking at me as if he thought me very cruel not to introduce him. He dances very well, and is such a nice fellow!"

"Oh, *thank* you!" said Miss Marlitt, with enthusiasm. She turned her pretty head, following the direction of Mrs. Boyce's glance to the door-way, in which a tall, yellow-haired young Yorkshireman stood talking with Miss Armory. The two were not saying very much, but it was certainly about Prudence Marlitt.

"I never saw so lovely a girl anywhere," pronounced honest Dick, with enthusiasm.

"There isn't any one in the room like her," said Helena Armory, "and I know you want to be introduced—only I don't know her."

"Well, she and your sister are great friends," said the young man.

"We will go over and melt Alice's heart, then," said Miss Armory, and accordingly she led the way toward Prudence. The introduction was quickly effected, and in a moment Prudence was among the dancers, being whirled stoutly around by the young Englishman. At first she protested she could not dance—as they did in England.

"But we know the 'Dip,'" pleaded Mr. Benison.

"The 'Dip?'" responded little Prudence. It so happened that Miss Marlitt was running about in short frocks on the beach at Ponkamak when the "Dip" went out of fashion in America.

"Well, then, let us try a *deux-temps*," said Dick; and Prudence, who was young and light-hearted, easily submitted to such a pleasant effort. Away they went. Mrs. Boyce and her sister, sitting against the peacock screen, and talking to half a dozen men, looked from time to time into the other room, where the girl's shabby muslin and beautiful face were constantly to be seen among the dancers. By this time Miss Armory was quite ready to announce herself as Prudence Marlitt's friend. The young lady had her usual circle of admirers, to whom she talked with that mixture of frankness and piquancy which made her charming. She knew a little of all the topics floating in the æsthetic circle, and a great deal of some of them, and she was keenly interested in everything people had to say. She had been long enough in England to feel herself in harmony with such traditions as affect society and every-day life, yet her American instincts were always apparent, giving a transatlantic flavor even to the way in which she wore her most æsthetic garments. Few English girls in society were more popular than Miss Armory, and her fortune was moderate enough to make the attentions paid her very complimentary. During part of the winter and in the regular season she and her sister, Mrs. Boyce, presided over a charming house in Cornwall Gardens, to which Americans were always cordially welcome, for neither of the two women had learned the art of patronizing her country people, while she assumed to be thoroughly one with them in feeling and tradition. During the hot months of the year Miss Armory was always with a cousin, who was keenly addicted to Continental travel; and for a certain number of weeks the young lady was to be found in two or three very fine country houses, where, though she never hunted, she was fond of riding, and was famous in the organization and performance of private theatricals. Mrs. Boyce's marriage, of course, had been the reason of her orphan sister's coming to live in England. Mr. Boyce was a wealthy Cornishman, who had met his charming wife while doing legation duty in Washington. Helena was only a girl of seventeen then, with silent, awkward beauty, and a fixed intention to be philanthropical. It was well known among her sister's friends that she had already refused two or three brilliant offers, and made the determination calmly never to marry. Whether English life had changed her views it was hard to say; she theorized a little more, and acted much less, and certainly never wilfully encouraged the men who had laid their hearts at her feet; but her manner had developed into self-possessed brilliancy. People declared her prettier and more fascinating than ever since æstheticism had crept across the land, but more inscrutable. "I don't know what it is she wants," Mrs. Boyce would say, with resignation, when asked by some interested lady friend why Helena did not marry.

"I am too worldly—that is it," Helena would always answer to such importunities. "Don't you see I love life so, I'm afraid of losing something by giving myself into a poor man's keeping—or an uninteresting man's—or a tyrannical man's—and then, I'm too worldly."

This was the young lady who, standing with a little circle of admirers about her at Mrs. Poynsett's, determined to assert herself as Prudence Marlitt's friend. She was rarely capricious, yet this sudden feeling of friendship was certainly impulsive.

"Mr. Simmonson," she said, sedately, to that

young man, "if you really wish to know Miss Marlitt well, you will have to be most attentive to me.
I am going to be a perfect Cerberus."

"Charming!" said Lord Bairham's heir. "Then
there will be double satisfaction in attentions to
Miss Marlitt."

"What an obvious compliment! All the same,
I suppose, I should have felt slighted if you had
neglected the chance. How does your Grosvenor
work go on?"

"Languidly," said Barley Simmonson, slowly.
"The subject has less — less of soul — than I
thought. Nothing responds, as it were, to the
feeling I put into the execution of the work."

"I wish I knew what to suggest," said Miss Armory. "Shall I come and read aloud Uhland to
you, or play Raff?"

"What a sweet idea!" said the young artist.
"That would be too delightful. Won't you
dance now, Miss Armory? Our waltz is half
over."

And so the young lady allowed herself to be
carried off to the dancers, where she passed Miss
Marlitt, radiant upon Dick Benison's arm.

Before the evening was over, the young girl from
Ponkamak, sternly chaperoned by Mrs. Boyce, had
made a multitude of friends, and given her address
a dozen times to different people. Mrs. Field Mowbray, whose Queen Anne house in Kensington is

an æsthetic centre, declared herself fascinated by the girl's beauty and charm of manner.

"My dear," she whispered to Miss Armory, "the child is like the Pompeiian Psyche."

Poor little Prudence! After the fashion among the "æsthetes" of the day, she was likened to every type of beauty since the days of our first parents. She was a Titian, a Bordone, a Botticelli—even a Sir Joshua and a Greuze. On the whole, Dick Benison came nearest to the truth when he called her, to Miss Armory, "a little darling." Mrs. Poynsett fully appreciated the success of Mrs. Boyce's *coup*. "But suppose," said the latter lady to her sister—"suppose they should turn out awful people to know—I mean the international copyright lady—what shall I do? And I never could pretend I didn't know the poor little thing after this."

Miss Armory declared she was not afraid. To her the whole charm of the evening resolved itself into watching or talking to Prudence. The way in which the girl received the attentions fluttering about her was beautiful. She had a smile, a bright word, a gay little laugh, always ready, and her cheek glowed with simple, heart-felt pleasure. The jargon of London society meant nothing to her. Was she a Bordone? a Titian? She may have heard the terms, but they implied nothing beyond civilities and kind heart.

"I think English people are perfectly *lovely*," she said once to Miss Armory. "And yet I always thought they would be so cold and reserved. But then you have been here so long."

"I've had five London seasons," said Miss Armory. "I love the people dearly," she added, with hearty meaning, and yet she would have liked to say a cynical word of warning to the girl beside her. Not for an instant did the homage paid her occur to the fresh young mind as subjective. Miss Armory would fain have guarded her from any chill, any disappointment, for she well knew how the girl's American mind was working. She danced two or three times with Mr. Simmonson, who succeeded better than young Benison in teaching her to waltz.

"In Ponkamak," she said to him once, in a breathless pause, "we dance the polka. Are you fond of it?"

Mr. Simmonson explained it was such an inartistic performance.

"Inartistic?" queried Prudence, lifting beautiful puzzled brows to the young man.

"Well, it has no purpose," he said, dreamily. "Now, Miss Marlitt, a waltz has its own power of harmonizing thought and movement. It is different."

Prudence stood still, not satisfied with herself, yet wondering what to say.

"Well," she said, finally, "I suppose Ponkamak
is countrified."

And then the two drifted on again, harmonizing
thought and movement charmingly, to judge by
Simmonson's rapt expression.

A little later Mrs. Boyce and Miss Armory carried Prudence away. In the dressing-room the girl
had an old seal-skin jacket and a faded pink worst-
ed cloud. Helena looked at the latter with a thrill
of remembrance. She could see herself, one of a
group of girls, at the Cliff House in L——, Con-
necticut, learning that stitch. What a boon the
stitch had been! After tea, she remembered, they
had all sat out on the piazza in crisp white gowns,
plying crochet-needles and comparing progress.
That evening, she remembered, the stage unexpectedly deposited Raymond De Kay, who had
come up, in spite of her silence, to see—the Cliff
House, he said. As Prudence Marlitt framed her
beauty in the worn bit of wool, Miss Armory stood,
across the room, a quiet, splendid figure in white
furs, with an expression few of her English friends
were familiar with. She wondered, as they made
their way into the hall, whether she were fifty instead of twenty-five.

Prudence's cavalier, Mr. Jonas Fielding, was waiting, and Miss Armory instantly regretted the slight
feeling of shame that she felt on beholding one of
the kindliest, truest-hearted men she ever knew.

But the typical Westerner is not ornamental in a
hall-way sombre with dull colors, lighted by wax-
candles and the flash of old brass and steel. Mr.
Jonas Fielding stood severely straight in a side
door-way against an Oriental portière. He was a
tall, well-built young man, with a fair, quiet face,
rather stiff light hair, and gentle blue eyes. He
typified the same part of the country, the same influences, which had produced this brilliant girl, with
her air of unconscious right to wear a coronet if
one were offered to her. They had been bred within sight of each other's door-ways, yet, as Miss Armory felt at once, for some subtle reason they were
as far asunder as the poles. Miss Armory did not
feel equal then to measuring any but the suggestive differences; she could not define Jonas Fielding beyond the momentary effect he produced;
yet in some ways the man's appearance startled
her.

He was a curious, forcible suggestion of home
—not the brilliant life of Washington, New York,
or Boston, which was in effect the life of London,
but the fervider, more intrinsically American life
which has for its background, as it were, the cañ-
ons of Colorado, the ranches of California. He oppressed Miss Armory with a miserable sense that
she had been in her heart of hearts guilty of some
forgetfulness. The subtlety of her feeling was
what puzzled her. Yet she knew that, were she

to meet the man a dozen times, she would hang her head for very shame.

The little "Bordone" went up to her friend with a lovely smile.

"How good of you, Jo!" she said, putting out one shabby glove. "I am so much obliged!" and then she turned and introduced him to Mrs. Boyce and Miss Armory. Mr. Fielding bowed and shook hands with each lady.

"Am I very late, Prue?" he said, gravely; but his mild eyes rested upon the girl as on some joyful object.

"Oh no," laughed Prudence. "I've had a perfectly *splendid* time. Mrs. Boyce and Miss Armory have been most kind. Do you know, Jo, it's awful here to go alone anywhere; and so Mrs. Boyce undertook to be my chaperon."

She laughed as she half whispered the words, and blushed prettily. As for the man, the color rushed into his face like a flame. For a moment he looked as if he would carry her away then and there.

"It is all right," said Mrs. Boyce. "I hope I may be her chaperon a great many times yet."

"Oh, thank you," said Jonas Fielding, in a deep, undemonstrative tone.

"Are you all fixed, Prue?" he asked, presently; and then, lightly, with a reverence which seemed to beautify the dingy color, he touched the pink cloud near her cheek.

Prudence gave a little extra tie to the cloud, and laughed and nodded. She was in beaming spirits. She exchanged fervent good-byes with Mrs. Boyce and Miss Armory, and begged they would call *early* the next day, and then she followed Jonas Fielding out into the winter starlight, where he had a cab in waiting. As the young man carefully led Prudence to the cab there was something quaintly chivalrous in his manner—his way of helping her to gather her limp draperies into one little gloved hand. Were they faded and poor to him? He touched the dingy folds with a gesture as of a knight kissing his lady's ribbon.

Driving toward Cornwall Gardens, Miss Armory was peculiarly despondent.

"I think it is the greatest pity in the world," she said at last, "that there should be *any* Jonas Fielding. Otherwise that girl might be a *perfect* success."

"She will be in spite of him," said Mrs. Boyce. "I *never* saw anything lovelier."

But in her own room, half an hour later, Miss Armory's despondency merged into something like melancholy.

"If I were a heroine in a novel," she thought, smiling to herself, "I would hunt up old love-letters and burn them. As it is, I am only "— the girl was sitting before her mirror, and she regarded herself dubiously—" only *what ?*" she thought ; and added, as she blew out her candle, " a modern ' æsthete ' !"

III.

PRUDENCE MARLITT and her aunt were in lodgings near Russell Square. Early the next day Mrs. Boyce's footman rapped at the door of the dull old house, and a maid-servant, down at the heel, and fragmentary as to cap and hooks and eyes, admitted Mrs. Boyce and Miss Armory. The maid carelessly led the way up to the front drawing-room, within which a clear American voice, like Prudence's grown thin, bade the visitors enter.

It was late in the autumn, yet, singular to say, not foggy, but the sitting-room looked dingy and comfortless in the extreme: a fire struggled in the grate; the usual ornaments under glass cases; antimacassars and prints vied with green and red furniture as depressing influences; but there was a piano open at the lighter end of the room, and from it Prudence, in a neat little walking-dress, was turning as the ladies came into the room. As Miss Armory kissed her, she encountered the brilliant gaze of a lady to whom Prudence smilingly introduced her new friends. Mrs. Crane was a woman of about forty, tall and dark, but handsome enough to show that beauty was a heritage among the Marlitts of Ponkamak; but she had none of Prudence's soft charm. She was thin, sharply cut, and decided in manner; and although she smiled a great deal, and with a very brilliant effect, her voice had the power of slowly reducing her hearers to subjection. Helena could always recall that morning visit accurately — the look of the room, the table littered with papers, the piano with Kücken's "Good-night" open upon it, the big windows through which the muffled tones of a street organ were to be heard, Prudence sitting in the shadow of the dreary fire, Mrs. Crane's eager glance at her guests—yet all strong impression seemed to be of that lady's voice as it went on and on, of her insistent personality, the movement of her thin, delicately moulded lips, her graceful domineering gestures.

"Prudence was very much obliged for your kindness last night," Mrs. Crane said, looking from one to the other of her visitors. "I'm sorry it wasn't the thing for her to go alone. The lady had been very kind. I don't know as I should have minded a girl's coming to my house just that way; still, each land has its laws. For myself, I claim individuality."

"English society is always very conventional outwardly," said Mrs. Boyce, smiling.

"Oh, I know." Mrs. Crane returned the smile

like the flash of steel. " The hollowest things can bear a strong outer glaze; but I feel our ideas are best. Still, I'm just as much obliged to you. I don't go out much in the evening myself."

" There are a great many social opportunities in the daytime," said Helena; " so many people receive between three and six."

" So I hear. Those are busy hours with me. You know I'm very much interested in public questions. I am to address a company at Lady Frances Holbrook's to-day." Mrs. Crane pronounced the title with a certain disdainful precision. " Not that her being what they call *Lady* over here makes any difference that I can see; but she is an *excellent* woman. I claim that a farmer's wife in America is equal to any 'Lady,' as they have it. I don't admit any social difference between the Queen and myself, and I think, if I met her to-morrow, I shouldn't give in to much bowing down."

Mrs. Boyce wondered if she had better answer this remark. She thought of one or two fitting speeches on the good-breeding of observing the etiquette of foreign countries; but Mrs. Crane's coldly brilliant gaze seemed to check the utterance of all opinions. She only said, " Is it to be a lecture this afternoon at Lady Frances's?"

" Well," said Mrs. Crane, with an elaborate manner, " I've been asked to give an account of our public schools in America, and I have prepared a paper to read on the subject. Are you interested in the question?"

"A little," Mrs. Boyce admitted. "But, you see, I've been six years away from home."

"But you read the papers—you know what is going on? Oh, Mrs. Boyce," exclaimed Mrs. Crane, putting her hands tightly together, "don't say you are one of those self-exiled American women who fall down at the feet of foreign aristocracy to worship, and forget their own country!"

Mrs. Crane, in uttering these impressive words, looked at the graceful figure of her visitor, taking in a swift impression of her charms, and I am afraid she measured her, although half-consciously, as the subject for "remarks" in Ponkamak. Certain phrases, indeed, flitted, half formed, through her mind: "An American lady, a beautiful, popular woman whom I met in London," etc.; or, "Few of our American women bear transplanting;" or, "English associations are taking so strong a hold upon our American women," etc.—various opening sentences occurred, as I say, to the lady's fertile mind while she looked at Mrs. Boyce's fair, delicate face, framed in the reddish-blonde hair and gray felt bonnet.

"What is that?" said Miss Armory, turning from her chat with Prudence by the fire.

"Mrs. Crane is disappointed in me," said Mrs.

Boyce. "But I hope you won't think all that of me, really. Do you know, although my husband is such a complete Englishman, and my children were both born here, I am considered a most rabid American. But one can be that, I hope, even in New York, and yet confess to ignorance of the public-school question. I can tell you all you like of art and literature and science over there; and I know a little bit about the President too!" Mrs. Boyce spoke with the most good-humored courtesy.

Mrs. Crane only answered by an earnest gaze at both Mrs. Boyce and Miss Armory: the younger lady had begun to be smilingly interested in Prudence Marlitt's aunt.

"Come to Lady Frances Holbrook's," said Mrs. Crane, with a gentle persistence. "I *know* you will be interested."

"Oh," said Miss Armory, "I am sure we should be, if we weren't engaged elsewhere. Lady Fanny is a great friend of ours, though I don't think she has ever quite forgiven me for laughing at her about something which happened in Paris last year. There was a meeting of ladies who discoursed on rights, and of course Lady Fanny was one of the principal people. You know how eager and earnest she is. She had a prominent place on the platform. We were in the audience, and I could see her plainly. She had been the prime mover in calling the meeting together, and all the speeches tended to prove that women can project themselves utterly into any public question, forgetting every minor point of feminine interest. I am sure the arguments were admirable. I was half determined to go home and declare new principles myself. Suddenly I saw Lady Fanny looking fixedly at me. Then she scribbled something on a bit of paper, and in a moment a boy brought it to me. It was about this: 'Dear Helena, I am in a perfect fidget. It is after four o'clock, and there is an *occasion* of pink foulard morning wrappers at the Louvre, and I know there won't be one left. I can't get away, and Janet dislikes to go, as Lord Roxburghley is going to speak, and he is sure to feel hurt if she leaves. Can you go over, dear, and secure for me *two*, and find out if all the white parasols are gone!' "

Mrs. Crane laughed—she could scarcely help it, indeed—yet her tone was not encouraging.

"Well," she said, "Lady Frances Holbrook seems earnest; but she is young and pretty, and I suppose a woman of fashion. What is an *occasion* ?" and Mrs. Crane's tone varied slightly. "Is the Louvre a good store—I mean for black silks?" she said, as Mrs. Boyce explained the term. "I wonder if Paris *is* the best place to shop in? But black silks are all chance now." Mrs. Crane grew a little more studious of Miss Armory's dark plush, and then she said : "This brings me to a question about Prudence, Mrs. Boyce. She needs to have some things bought, if she's to go out any more in this English society, and your advice would be valuable. From what she tells me, they dress very oddly here in company, but she says it's pretty. Really, if you *could* direct her a little. I should like her to have everything nice. Last night it was all done in such a hurry, just anything she'd chanced to bring over."

Now, when people met Prudence Marlitt later, it was always a source of astonishment how the girl had so quickly learned the art of æsthetic dress. Mrs. Boyce and her sister never told the story of that morning's expedition; how they carried the girl off in triumph to Regent Street, and to Burnett's and Madame J——'s, and bought those pretty gowns, the long cloak, the big felt hat, which made Prudence more than ever bewitching. The shabby muslin was packed away, and before Mrs. Boyce's famous *conversazione* on December 20, Prudence had a gown of shining satin, devised by Miss Armory in what she considered her most æsthetic moment.

"But one can't help thinking," Helena remarked to her sister, "what Jonas Fielding will say to it."

"What do you care?"

"A great deal," answered Helena. "I'm afraid—though I don't know why—he will think her crazy."

"Then let him find out his mistake," said Mrs. Boyce. The two were matching wools in South Kensington, and Helena became very critical of the green shades offered for inspection.

"It will never seem a mistake to him," she said, with a sigh, "and there's the pity of it. This will do, Alice, I think. Now I mean to make those leaves perfect. Oh, what a joy it is!"

Before the evening of the *conversazione* in Cornwall Gardens, Miss Armory made a discovery which delighted her. Going into the dingy sitting-room in Guildford Street one day, she found Prudence singing, and it ensued that the girl possessed a lovely voice. The compass was not great, but it was a clear mezzo, full of impassioned cadence— such tones as our Western nightingales often unconsciously possess.

"The very thing to complete her character here!" Helena thought, as she drove home that afternoon. "Oh, if Jonas Fielding were only miles away!"

But he was much nearer. Indeed, half his time seemed to be spent in Guildford Street, where his broad shoulders were constantly to be seen darkening the window, while Mrs. Crane wrote letters, and Prudence worked in the fire-light. Sometimes Miss Armory encountered him on the dusky staircase as she came up or down. He was unfailing in his attentions to his friends; he performed endless little services for them with a quiet, manly air that took away all idea of slavery; once Helena declared she met him bringing in cold chicken.

"Horrible!" said Mrs. Boyce.

"Well, perhaps it wasn't quite that," answered Miss Armory; but it was something to eat—oranges, perhaps."

"Can't you forgive the man for existing?" Mrs. Boyce declared.

"No, I can't," said her sister. "He is my 'Old Man of the Sea.' I wonder how I can shake him off?"

IV.

MISS ARMORY, in declaring that Jonas Fielding was her "Old Man of the Sea," gave rather exaggerated expression to the estimate she had, half-consciously, made of the man's power. Something about him, awkward and reserved as he seemed, impressed her as worth considering, and in inducting Prudence into the ways of the "æsthetes," she felt as if she, in some fashion, owed him an apology. But Miss Armory's mind was, as she knew herself, morbidly analytical. She was given to taking out her opinions and dissecting and elaborating them for her own amusement, in a way that perhaps even Mrs. Boyce would not understand; she was perpetually commenting to herself on the motive of the most commonplace actions; she declared herself without a creed, yet she was haunted by a sense that a conscience was one of the grandest things appertaining to human nature, and that it needed some unseen awful guidance. In the fine, high-bred face of the girl one read this critical, self-reproachful faculty; it was in the curve of her lips, the glance of her dark eyes. She had an almost passionate sense of justice, and was perpetually telling herself that her whole life was an imposition upon her better self; yet nothing in the world pleased her nearly so well as the close association with the world of poetry, pictures, and color in its varied forms which was called "æsthetic London." Introducing Prudence Marlitt into this visionary region afforded Helena the keenest delight; but as the evening of Mrs. Boyce's *conversazione* approached, she declared she felt it was not altogether merciful.

"I am not rendering unto Jonas the things that are Jonas's," she said to Mrs. Boyce, in an indolent moment, when they were taking tea together in Helena's dressing-room.

"I wouldn't be wicked, and strike my breast together," said Alice Boyce.

"Oh yes you would, if you were me," said Helena. "Don't you know I always do, and I take a grim pleasure in my power of dissecting my own wickedness. I wonder what I am the result of—some intense Puritanism, and modern American infidelity—and it's so horrible to feel one's self so real!"

Mrs. Boyce, for all her æstheticism, had calm, old-fashioned views on religion.

"If you were a Roman Catholic, you'd be a Trappist," she said, laughing.

"I know I should. Sometimes I think I will be —after I've finished being an 'æsthete.'"

As for Prudence herself, she appeared to have no doubt at all about the fitness of her appearance at Mrs. Boyce's *conversazione* in the shining satin, short-waisted and short-sleeved, with her hair coiled high in those careless waves which we see in old pictures, wondering at the craft of our grandmothers' handmaidens. She came early, as Mrs. Crane was at Lady Fanny's, and "received" with her two friends. She was a little startled by the exquisite beauty of the rooms, for so far she had only seen the house in Cornwall Gardens in dusky moments and dull weather. Mrs. Boyce's house is not too large a one to have pretty rooms, yet there is given an idea of space : doors give way to portières, width is cherished, corners are not overcrowded. The drawing-room is full of comfort as well as beauty. There are tranquil places in it, with deep window-seats, soft carpets, the repose of some good picture or dainty bit of blue. No one is ever wearied in that drawing-room ; the colors seem to have gathered there of themselves—a slow procession, as it were—tributes to the harmonies of the house ; and whatever of art or decoration there is, is of the best. Prudence seemed thoroughly to fit her surroundings, and Miss Armory, whose spirits rose as the rooms filled and æstheticism was heavy on the air, forgot to cry " Peccavi." The girl was utterly lovely in her dainty gown. She had a rich cluster of yellow roses in her belt, soft frills of yellowish lace in her neck and sleeves, and long white Swedish gloves. The effect was perfect, and Miss Armory, when the first hour of receiving was over, sat down in the embrasure of a window, amused and interested by the sensation the girl was creating. Prudence had her circle of admirers very soon, but she sat and talked very gayly, betraying no special interest in any peculiar features of the scene. The names of certain famous people, painters and scholars and musicians, had awakened a keen though momentary interest in her; but Miss Armory could not decide whether the picturesqueness appealed to anything responsive in her, or whether it only amused her—whether she "believed" in the cut of her own lovely gown, or whether she thought she had "dressed up." It was hard, indeed, to tell just what effect this concentrated London would produce on her concentrated Americanism.

While Miss Armory was puzzling over the subtleties this involved, Prudence glanced at her with a dimpling smile, and Helena observed Barley Simmonson approaching them. As this young man has something especial to do with my story, I am afraid I must say a few words regarding him. He was a young man born and bred to such expectations that it would be cruel to criticise his indolence and various peculiarities. At thirty he had tired of the usual occupations of noble youth, and turned, for amusement and occupation, to art and poetry, doing most in the former: painting all the pretty women of society in water-colors with a sort of air which people were pleased to call charming. "A Barley Simmonson" was already talked about, and Kensington and Bond Street shop-windows displayed his "heads," while Lord Bairham spoke of "my nephew—the artist, you know—Simmonson." Mr. Simmonson was regarded as an authority where Intensity and Soul were concerned, and his countenancing a thing made it acceptable, though some people, like Miss Armory, were inclined to say he needed a check. "If I were to let Barley Simmonson crawl about the rug of my sitting-room," this young lady once said, in calm opposition to laudatory remarks upon his ease of manner, "I should be as much ashamed of myself as I was of him. It's all very well to have temperament, but Mr. Simmonson need not lie down on the floor when he reads poetry to me." It was this young man who, with a certain melancholy grace, approached Prudence, and, as it were, seemed prepared to pose his lurid Intensity against her fresh, unaffected, unthinking nature.

V.

PRUDENCE was delighted to see a young man whom she had met before.

"Oh, *how* do you do, Mr. Simmonson?" she said, and held out her long, wrinkled glove prettily. Mr. Simmonson took the girl's fingers, holding them a moment as though he were imprisoning something precious.

"I hope Miss Marlitt is well," he said, smiling.

Prudence nodded.

"Oh, *very*," she added, drawing a little quick breath of satisfaction. "But then, I am *always* well." She laughed, dimpling and coloring like a June rose. She looked utterly lovely, and Mr. Simmonson was not too much engrossed by the thought surging, or, as he would have said, "pulsating," within him, to observe it.

"Health is certainly a blessing," he said, sinking into a chair near Prudence and Miss Armory. "I never go into my own county—Somerset—without envying the peasant his vigor—envying, that is, in a subjective way." Prudence's alert brightness was a little clouded, but she listened intently. "I like to see the peasant at his work. I like to imagine

how he feels, walking up a brown hill—the furze
in feathery outline, the sky streaked with red and
gray lines—"

"But does he care for the sky?" said Prudence,
gayly.   Mr. Simmonson looked at her with a pen-
sive smile.

"But I like him better with these surroundings,"
he said, gently insistent.   "It is *then* his vigor appeals to me: given the picturesqueness of a Somerset heath, a windy day, and that plodding, up-
ward-toiling figure excites my strongest pulsations
—then his vigor is not repulsive."

"Repulsive!" echoed little Prue.   She smiled,
but looked troubled.   "I didn't suppose *vigor* had
anything *repulsive* in it."

"Abstractly, of course," assented Barley.   "Yet
muscle can be repulsive.   Who can be *soulful* and
an athlete?   The *mind* never succeeds unless the
body suffers."

"Is that so?" said Prudence, as though Mr.
Simmonson were pronouncing a medical opinion.
"Yet I have a particular friend—Jonas Fielding,
you know, Miss Armory—and if his lungs were
only stronger, he'd be a real success as a preacher,
every one says.   He *looks* well enough, but he's
had pneumonia two winters.   He used to be a
Methodist, but he's changed his views; he's a
Congregationalist now—at least, a *sort* of Congregationalist.   I don't think he accepts quite all

they do. At one time he was very near being a
Unitarian; but anyway he's a real believer, and
oh! it's *such* a pity his lungs are weak! He was
smarter than any one in my brother's class at Andover or Yale."

Prudence's sweet eyes had real light in them,
but the effect of her gentle, rapid utterances was
to set Mr. Simmonson dreamily communing with
himself. The figure of Jonas Fielding, quondam
Methodist, full of genuine meaning and real life,
as opposed to his visionary peasant toiling upward
against a red-streaked sky, made the conversation
uninteresting. He sat still a moment, leaning one
arm on the back of his chair, his eyes absently
resting on Prudence, whose outlines seemed gradually to impress him anew.

"The flesh comes wonderfully with that satin,"
he said, earnestly.

Prudence gave a little start.

"I wish you would sit for me, Miss Marlitt.
Your head is perfect." Mr. Simmonson's eyes
were mere lines between their fair lashes as he
looked at the girl. "The drawing about the chin,
too, is wonderfully fine." He waved a significant
thumb. "Couldn't you get Mrs. Boyce and Miss
Armory to come with you to my studio? I would
give much for some impression of you as you look
to-night."

What might have been Prudence's answer it is

impossible to say.   By this time Miss Armory was
engaged in conversation with two or three people
on the other side of her, but she heard Mr. Simmonson's request.   As she flashed an amused, in-
quisitive glance around at Prudence, she beheld
Mrs. Crane approaching.   Mrs. Crane was expensively dressed in a black silk, about which there
were a great many frills and fringes, and a suggestion of Sunday church-going as well as tea-parties.
Her hair was done up in a myriad of finger puffs.
She wore some very good Valenciennes lace in her
neck and sleeves.   As she crossed the room she
dispensed brilliant glances right and left.   She
was evidently in the very height of good spirits.
By the time she shook hands with Miss Armory
she was positively laughing.

   " Well !" she said, standing before Prudence ;
and, after a brief glance at her niece, she swept
the room again with her gold eye-glass ; then she
brought her amused glance back to Prudence,
whose charming gown she studied critically.
" Isn't it ridiculous ?" she said, very good-humoredly—" *ridiculous !*"

   Miss Armory offered no defence of her pet opinions, and Prudence only looked at her aunt with a
sweet beseeching eagerness.   She wanted that absorbed lady to participate in her pleasure in the
evening.   Mrs. Crane's eyes had scanned Mr. Simmonson for a few seconds before Prue whispered

to Helena, " Do introduce this funny gentleman to
Aunt Rebecca," and Miss Armory had taken what
seemed to her a most interesting suggestion.   Mr.
Simmonson had already risen, and was standing
beside his chair when Miss Armory made the introduction.   Helena was much entertained by observing the two together, exchanging greetings.
If one wanted a study of types, it was assuredly to
be found here.   The American lady intensely, eagerly alert, as conscious of herself and her " cause "
as Barley Simmonson. was of a " temperament "
and a " soul ;" each embodied something so peculiarly belonging to their period that the meeting
might have been recorded as a picture of the time,
a suggestion of thought, fancy, or feeling in a human form.   But as actual fact, there was only a
commonplace hand-shaking—a few words, while
Mrs. Crane dangled her eye-glass, and Barley Simmonson looked out from the heavy locks of light
hair which fell upon his brow.   In a moment his
glance returned to the " flesh effects " above Prudence's shining gown.

"I've just been asking Miss Marlitt to sit for
me, Mrs. Crane," he said, softly; "I want to paint
her head."

Mrs. Crane was again sweeping the room
through her glass.

"Yes?" she said.   She smiled abstractedly, and
seemed to nod an assent.   In a moment she passed

her smile on to Miss Armory. "Browning was at Lady Frances Holbrook's to-night," she said; "I was *so* glad to meet him!"

By this time Mr. Simmonson had begun a low-toned conversation with Miss Marlitt. Helena proposed to Mrs. Crane to make the tour of the rooms, and in so doing the latter's brilliant gaze fell upon Dr. Huxfell. She was speedily engrossed in a talk with him, and Helena wandered on, making a few introductions here and there, stopping for light piquant remarks to one or another of the people, who were all ready enough to talk to Mrs. Boyce's charming sister. By this time the music was fairly under progress, and it had come Prudence's turn to sing. Two young ladies had given an abrupt little German duet, beginning on a shrill high note, and ending in about half a moment with a cry of despair. The usual "Ohs" and "Ahs" were uttered; one lady, not far from Prudence, convulsively caught her companion by the arm, sinking her head in her shoulders, and allowing tears to course unchecked down her cheeks. Hergliebe, standing near Miss Armory, glanced at her in a sort of horror. When Prudence Marlitt stood up to sing, he expected nothing better; but I think he will always remember the impression she created, the picture she made. She stood by the piano, a shining figure against the darkly polished floor, the sombre tints of the room. Her head was daintily poised; the roses in her belt hung in a rich cluster; above her shone a mild radiance of candle-light, which seemed to vibrate in the dusky places, making even her rich beauty more fair.

Had the girl, in reality, all that unuttered, unutterable longing within her? She sung as though something in her heart was breaking. It was a little Finnish ballad, almost unknown in London. There was not despair—only simple, untutored feeling in it, and Prudence could interpret primitive meanings. She attempted no elaborate expression. Her lips parted in pure, delicious sound, and the sweet nature of the girl was in every note.

While Prudence was singing, Helena became conscious of a new presence just beside her, and looked up to see Jonas Fielding's tall figure, a shadow in the door-way. He smiled upon Miss Armory, who was conscious of a sudden desire to watch him; but he turned his gaze almost at once, and with eager intentness, upon Prudence.

The faintest shadow of surprise, that might have deepened into pain, crossed the man's face. He had pictured Prudence in so many ways—there seemed in his mind a precedent for anything she might do or say, or even seem to be; but never before had he thought of her fashioned thus, or in such surroundings. It was scarcely so much a

revelation to him as it was a curious phase of life
newly presented to him, with Prudence—*his* Prudence—for a centre-piece.   A strange look gathered in his eye.   He was trying to accustom himself
to what jarred upon his earlier remembrances—
what made association painful—what tinged his
.simple faith with a distrust of which he felt afraid.
He stood quite still while she sung, now and then
beating time on his chin with one hand; but the
music meant little to him.   Almost before she had
finished, he bent down and half whispered to Miss
Armory,

"Did you ever hear Prudence sing 'Nearer, my
God, to Thee'?"

A quiet smile flickered into his eyes—a look of
one who, in the midst of many sounds, recalls the
tenderness of some vibrating long-ago.

Helena returned his confidential glance.

"No," she whispered back; "but she must sing
it some day for me.   It is a great favorite of
mine."

"Yes," he said, and made a gesture which, rather scornfully, included the whole company—" of
course it wouldn't do here."

Helena nodded, and swept away her white draperies that Fielding might take a place beside her.
He looked pleasantly at her, and was rather struck
by her very delicate good looks.   Miss Armory's
type was distinctively American, yet she might

have belonged to the French court a century ago. She had the clearly cut features, expressive mouth, and dark eyes which we are accustomed to associate with beauties of the eighteenth century. Her hair was richly brown. There was a grace even in the thin curves of her face—certainly nothing meagre in her outlines, and the delicacy seemed only of type, for her coloring was a clear, healthful white. What was lacking in regular beauty she certainly made up for in brilliancy and expression. Her mouth was rather wide, but her smile was perfect, and her voice had a pure, clear tone, which, though it had never acquired the undulations of the English voice, was pronounced charming by the most Saxon of her friends.

Fielding sat down by Miss Armory, but, after his first gratifying glance at her profile, he let his thoughts drift away. By this time Prudence's song was ended, and people were roused to very audible enthusiasm. The girl had a little court about her. Fielding looked at her with a strained sort of expression, pleased and yet perplexed. Of what period in their lives was he thinking? Helena, looking at him half furtively, fancied she could read his thoughts. She knew just what he and Prudence might have been in Ponkamak. She could see the cheerful parlor in which the girl might have read with him or sung for him—its homely attractions, the fancy-work, the stiff sofas, the piano and melodeon, the good engravings, and the well-lined book-shelves. She could see them in such a room, lamplit and curtained cosily against the cruelty of an Eastern winter; the girl, beautiful, sweet-tempered, and charming; the man merging his Methodistical fervor into broader planes, something in his mind or nature, as it wrestled with spiritual problems, needing the warmth and beauty of her companionship. As years drifted on, thought Helena, he may have come to know that this girl was all his world, that she fulfilled all his unspoken longings. He analyzed nothing, for he accepted everything; and now, now he sat there only demonstrating, by that strange look in his eyes, the slow beating of the sinewy fingers on his chin, that he feared he should lose her utterly in a chaos of hateful sound and color and movement, for which his life in its most unfettered moments offered no precedent.

Prudence, from among her admirers, drifted toward Miss Armory, flushed and pleased. She laughed, a little nervously, as she saw Jonas.

"Well, Prue!" he said, in his kind voice.

She nodded her head, smiling, and drawing one or two long breaths of pleasure.

"I was frightened when I began," she said to him. "Did I show it?"

"No, dear; it was beautiful."

These were almost the only words they exchanged that evening. Prudence was sought for on all sides, and Jonas Fielding withdrew into the inner library—a sort of sanctum of Mr. Boyce's, where the newest as well as the oldest in literature was to be found. The young man had occupied some time in examining the backs of the books, when Miss Armory discovered him alone, but with no dejection in his manner.

"You must let me introduce you to some one," she said, pleasantly.

"Thank you," Fielding said, simply. But Miss Armory stood irresolute a moment, a graceful figure leaning against the dark book-shelves, and moving a big white fan slowly.

"What kind of people do you like?" she said, looking at him good-humoredly.

Fielding smiled.

"Have you all kinds?" he said, and glanced through the portières to the crowded rooms beyond, where everything was light and movement and sound. Even as he did so he came back, with a grateful sense of repose, to Miss Armory's charming figure and delicate face.

"Almost all kinds," she said, laughing; "but let me make a choice for you. I wonder if I shall do it well?"

She looked at Jonas with almost tender inquiry in her eyes. There is no mode of flattering man or woman so sure as that which insinuates a knowledge of personal opinions or feelings, but Miss Armory had not the vaguest idea of being personal in what she looked or said. If she had any motive it was a half-formed one, prompted by that sense of treason toward Jonas Fielding which had lurked in her mind since the day at Burnett's with Prudence. There was also an undefined longing to understand the motive of the man's life and thought, and to see if she underrated it. But Jonas Fielding saw only kindness and courtesy and a certain something that was pleasing in the girl's soft glance.

"I shall introduce you to Lady Ericson," she said, mentioning a famous traveller's wife; "I know you and she will like each other," and so saying she led the way from Mr. Boyce's room. But just beyond the curtains she stopped with another brilliant glance at Fielding. "I want you to come and see me especially," she said. "I am always at home between eleven and one in the morning; now don't forget it!"

Jonas assured her he would not, and before she made the promised introduction she removed one more burden from her conscience. "I want also to have you know Barley Simmonson, the artist," she said. "Prudence Marlitt has agreed to sit to him." To this Jonas said nothing, but he gave Miss Armory a searching look.

VI.

JONAS FIELDING left Mrs. Boyce's *conversazione* determined to seek an early opportunity of accepting Miss Armory's invitation. That young lady had impressed him as wide-minded in the midst of confusing influences. There was certainly something pleasing, as well as perfectly sincere, in her frank gaze and manner of treating him. He felt a degree of satisfaction in her society which made him forget any of the reasons for embarrassment or distaste which oppressed him in English society, and he believed that she could offer him frank and simple solutions of the social problems which already disquieted him. Accordingly, he made his appearance in Cornwall Gardens one morning about five days after Mrs. Boyce's *conversazione*, and was pleased to find Miss Armory alone in the sitting-room or boudoir devoted to her special use. She looked uncommonly pretty. She was becomingly dressed in dark green, although to Jonas the color and intention of picturesqueness seemed slightly theatrical; but he thought the general effect not unpleasant. She was embroidering as he came in, and quickly put down a heap of white-and-gold and dull-red silks upon a table near her.

"I am so glad to see you, Mr. Fielding," she said, cordially. "I felt sure you would come soon."

"Yes," said Jonas, smiling in his shrewd, reflective way, "I made up my mind that you meant it."

"Of course I meant it. Now do sit down and make yourself comfortable."

But Jonas appeared to prefer leaning against the chimney-piece.

"Well," said Miss Armory, "I never interfere with that attitude in a man. Men always appear to derive a special satisfaction from chimney-pieces. I'm sure fireplaces never ought to go out of fashion."

Although Miss Armory laughed, it was without any of the air of having made one of the abstract speeches of society, and Jonas, who had no sense of piquant repartee, answered nothing for a moment. Then:

"Yes," he said, slowly, "I am fond of standing up. I think, if you've anything on your mind, it is easier to say it standing up or walking about."

"Then you shall do as you like, and, if you try, I think you could walk about even this confused little room."

"Is it confused?" Jonas said, good-humoredly. He looked about the many artistic decorations and furnishings, which indeed nearly filled the room, but, as in the drawing-room, there were certain wide, tranquil spaces. "I don't think I shall have to walk about much," he said, smiling; "but I think I could make my way. I hope you won't get tired of me."

"No, I promise that. May I go on with my work?" and Miss Armory gathered up the rich mass of color at her side.

"What is that?" asked Jonas, politely. "I suppose it is for a fair. Ladies do a great deal of worsted-work now, don't they? Is that a tidy?"

"Yes," said Miss Armory, slowly; she drifted back some years at the mention of the forgotten name. "They call them antimacassars and sofa-backs here."

"Do they?" Jonas looked a moment at the deftly moving fingers and the colors, which he felt harmonized perfectly with all the surroundings, yet by means of some subtle power he could not define. "Miss Armory," he said, a little suddenly, "I've come to talk to you about something very particular. It's about Prudence."

Miss Armory nodded. "Yes; I knew you had."

"Well, I suppose Prudence is in English society now?"

"Yes, Mr. Fielding; and, do you know, I am sure she is going to be a genuine success. That is something worth attaining in this worn-out day."

"Worn out!"—the young man laughed unaffectedly. "Worn out!" he repeated, with almost a pitying glance at the girl before him.

"Yes, Mr. Fielding, worn out in certain ways. You carry your atmosphere of freshness and clearness so strongly about with you that I can't talk to you much about it."

"Oh, go on," he pleaded; "I beg you will."

"Well, then, you don't know how Fashion has tired herself, how glad she is of the *raison d'être* in—well, in this very tidy I am doing. People are still seeking novelty."

"What is it that they want?"

"I am not sure they know themselves. But there is one thing certain, in many things a great degree of perfection is required."

"Are there grades of perfection in anything, Miss Armory?"

"Well, there are different kinds, I should say; or, rather, we see perfection little by little. Nowadays people want to see a great deal, however, at once. English society is charming and beautiful and artistic, and in certain circles splendid, but it is in some ways what our friend Mrs. Crane would call—hollow."

Miss Armory laughed, but she saw that Jonas listened intently.

"Go on," he said, very gravely. "Tell me sincerely about it. How do these people"—he waved his hand as if including the phantoms of the other night—"how do these people think and feel and live?"

"How am I to tell you?" said Miss Armory, looking at him with a little uncomfortable laugh. "I am only philosophizing, please remember. And as you are a clergyman, you will be telling me presently that I ought not to judge people by surface indications."

"If you will be candid, and give me the benefit of your knowledge, Miss Armory, you need not be afraid I shall preach to you."

"Well, then, these people—pray remember I am one of them myself—undertake to set up standards of *feeling*. It is all very well to use Chelsea teacups and old blue, to wear olive-green and dead gold, because it is the fashion—all that comes of our keener appreciations of good form and color; but when you are told just how your pulses should beat, what should reach your inmost being, what folly you may indulge in because it expresses *soul*, then I say it is time to grow philosophical."

Miss Armory was working languidly. She did not look at Jonas when she ceased speaking, but the young man sought her gaze. He looked at her intently.

"And to be a *success?*" he said, sharply.

Miss Armory lifted her eyes. "To be a success in this circle," she answered, "is to contribute to the beauty, the brilliancy, the magnetism, or the *effect* of the hour."

Jonas remained silent. He looked around as though he might begin that impetuous walking about of which he had spoken; but in fact no repose was more complete than that expressed by his tall, sinewy figure leaning against the chimney-piece. "I am afraid," he said at last— "I am afraid I do not receive new impressions quickly."

Miss Armory smiled, and held out her hands with an expressive gesture.

"I don't think it is *that*," she said, earnestly. "It is because—don't you see?—it's like expecting to understand an unknown tongue in an hour. Indeed, I only half know it myself. Wait until you hear it talked a little longer around you."

"No," said Fielding, "it isn't *that* either. I am not one of those to be enlightened ever by it. He stopped a moment, and then added, with an air of shrewd conviction, "I don't like it."

Miss Armory continued to look at him earnestly.

"Wait!" she said, brilliantly.

"Ah!" exclaimed Fielding, smiling, "you are pleading the cause of this—this sort of thing yourself, after all you have said."

"What did I say?" she answered, eagerly. "Did I say I didn't like it? Oh, I know I analyzed it; but don't you know there are times, and especially with certain people, when we analyze and criticise our deepest, our dearest beliefs?"

Jonas smiled thoughtfully.

"Well," he said, growing preoccupied again, "this is not what I meant to say of Prudence."

"No," it is not, and even now I don't know what to say of her. I told you she was going to be a success, and so she is."

"To contribute to the beauty, the brilliancy, the magnetism, or the effect of the hour?" said the young man, without a tinge of irony in his tone. The sedate intensity of his manner impressed Miss Armory. She paused; she had abandoned her work, but she moved the silks through her fingers carefully.

"Not the magnetism," she answered.

"Why not?" Jonas spoke in a low tone.

"Well, I don't want to answer you hastily, though I promise to be more explicit in the future. All I can say at the moment is, she wouldn't know how."

"Oh, then," exclaimed the young man, with a light laugh, "that is an acquired art here, is it? Well, Prudence may learn."

Miss Armory shook her head.

"Not if she stayed here forever; it isn't in her; but she will be just as successful in another way. She is so divinely beautiful."

"Prudence is a handsome girl," answered Jonas,

almost as though defending her against the charge of too æsthetic a beauty. "In Ponkamak every one thought so."

"Then she is accustomed to success?"

"Ah," exclaimed Jonas, with a quiet tone of sadness, I shall have to explain *our* meanings to you, Miss Armory. In Ponkamak Prudence was respected and loved."

"She is respected here, Mr. Fielding, and loved in just the same sort of way. Of course I know just what you mean; but don't you realize the difference between a large circle and a small one? In Ponkamak every one had grown up with every one else. There was no question of sudden ideas, of revelations in beauty or acquirements; here society has only time to look on in a surface way. It is never sure of renewing any phase of feeling a second season. The sweetness of constant remembrance and association must be lacking."

"You all seem to be remarkably intimate," said Jonas, gravely. "That young Simmonson, for instance, the artist, why, I heard him talking to half a dozen people as if they were his dearest friends."

Miss Armory smiled, and again made that little, despairing gesture with her hands.

"That is part of the language. You must learn to be one of them," she said, laughing. "But don't let us be abstract any more, Mr. Fielding. There is something I want much to know. Tell me about Prudence. Have you known her long?"

"Always," he answered; and there drifted across his remembrance a picture of baby Prudence on his shoulder as he tramped through the snow; of the child Prudence watching for him on his way from school; of the girl Prudence, tall and beautiful, but still trustfully dependent. With these pictures came the framework of simple home life— clear beliefs, clear purposes. They carried him easily down to the present hour, but here they seemed to stand still, veiled, obscured, mystified by the newer settings, beyond which he strove in bewilderment to believe in the past.

"Always," he repeated. "Her brother was my dearest friend. We went to school together in Ponkamak, and we went to Andover the same day; but there Marlitt shot clear ahead of me. Everything there, as I remember it, seems to have belonged to him. I was a shy sort of boy, and he made life open treasures to me. Prudence is beautiful. Well, his mind was like Prue's face. I never saw anything like what he absorbed of the best in everything. He had a nature you couldn't be near without feeling; and, for all his study and science, he had the heart of a boy. Well, we both began to study for the ministry together; but while I was plodding on the ground, Marlitt had thought out all his spiritual life. He had lifted himself up to

the highest places. Marlitt—" Jonas Fielding
paused; his theme seemed to have made him for-
getful of everything else, yet he could not find
words. "Marlitt," he repeated, intensely, and with
the look of some suffering long held dumb in his
eyes, "I *cannot* believe that death could kill him."

"And he died?" Miss Armory said, gravely.

Jonas inclined his head.

"Yes. It was the time of the yellow-fever in
New Orleans. He went down there: he felt he
must. He died after months of toil, weary in the
harness. I was always glad he had accomplished
something, and I found he had left his impress
upon many minds. He was *real*, but to me he is
one of the incontrovertible arguments against an-
nihilation: everything half uttered; all that subtle
brain-power; the depth of heart-meaning; the unspoken; the undefined; yet the rich, rich possibility. Can it be it is gone, broken and unfinished,
ended forever beneath a few feet of sod? What
demon could have created such an earth?"

After a moment Miss Armory said, in a low tone,
"And Prudence?"

Jonas passed his hand across his forehead. He
was still leaning against the chimney-piece, but he
had ceased while he talked to look at Miss Armory. His eyes were fixed upon the bit of wintry
Park visible through the window.

"Yes, Prudence," he said. "She was his idol.

He would talk of her by the hour. Of all things he had dreaded for her was "—the young man turned a quick gaze toward Miss Armory, toward the room, toward, as it were, the London which was making Prudence a success—" was *this—this*."

" Do you think if he had known—" Miss Armory was beginning, when Jonas checked her :

" He knew all human nature ; nothing was too wide, too remote, for him. You can study all the world, he used to say, if you like, in six people. He understood Prudence, and he loved her. Miss Armory, listen to me. If you make Prudence a success here, she will *not* be one at home among the people who truly love her."

Miss Armory was standing up herself now. She had begun to move rather restlessly about the room. " I have nothing to do with it," she said, finally, stopping short before the young man, and looking at him with a compassionate gaze.

" You called yourself one of them a while ago," he said, bitterly.

Miss Armory looked down at the fire, twirling an ornament of her châtelaine in her fingers. " This is morbid," she said at last. " You will see it for yourself later. I repeat again, Mr. Fielding—*wait*."

" How long ?" he asked, gravely.

" Oh," returned Miss Armory, trying to laugh, "I have no idea of suggesting a dissection of society in regard to its effects upon Prudence, nor of asking you to look on at a few scenes from a metaphysical point of view. Believe I am only anxious to see you less unhappy."

"I am not unhappy."

"You are apprehensive and suspicious, which is a great deal worse; and you are starting out to judge of us on a morbid, prejudiced basis. When you came in first, I thought I had penetrated your feelings—your point of view seemed so apparent— but I see now that I was mistaken."

"I am not one of you," said the young man, with a kind of gloomy insistence.

"Don't harbor that against me. Come, Mr. Fielding; I am truly Prudence's friend, and I want to be yours. Won't you believe me when I tell you that you are allowing yourself to be morbid?"

He shook his head.

"She is a curious girl," he said, slowly. "Marlitt was right in saying she should have her foundations firmly fixed before any strong wave swept over her."

"And you think she has come into what you call *this* too crudely?"

"She will be dazzled," he said, gravely.

"And why not? A dazzle is often a very good thing."

"No!" He spoke a general negative, but Miss Armory was keen enough to understand its special application.

"Then why don't you say all this to her your-self?" she exclaimed.

Jonas smiled sadly.

"Surely you see," he said. "How much of all this would she understand?"

It was certainly a tribute to Miss Armory's intui-tions, but she scarcely thought of that.

"Then what am I to do?" she said, with calm despair. "Remember, I think you morbid."

"We have drifted so far away from the begin-ning of this talk," said Jonas, "that you forget the impression you were willing to convey half an hour ago."

"Oh," said Miss Armory, "half an hour ago! I didn't know you then."

"You don't know me yet," said Jonas, a little sadly; "nor even does my poor little Prudence. I am going to use your word, Miss Armory," and he smiled good-humoredly—"*wait!*"

He held out his hand for good-bye, and the girl very quickly put her own in it. It was odd that this ungainly, unimpressive young man should be leaving her with a sense of defeat, or at least a de-sire to make herself appreciated and better under-stood. While he held her hand in a thoroughly impersonal sort of way, she was swiftly trying to think of some way to prolong the talk, or bring about another interview.

"I shall quote you, then," she said, finally, clasp-

ing her hands and looking at him very brilliantly:
" How long?"

Jonas smiled shrewdly. " Until I say, Enough,"
he answered.

There was a moment's silence, after which Miss
Armory said, " Have you accepted Mr. Simmonson's invitation to his studio?"

" Of course. I went there yesterday."

" Indeed! and what did you do?"

" You can imagine. I looked at his pictures,
and he talked."

" Did he? I don't think you appreciate your
privileges. Mr. Simmonson is considered a most
desirable acquaintance."

" I am going again to-morrow, to lunch with him."

Miss Armory involuntarily stared.

" I am studying him," said Jonas Fielding, " and
I think he is studying me."

Miss Armory knew she should enjoy reflecting
upon this later.

" Well," she said, " then I suppose we shall meet
you there at the sittings?"

" I hope so," he said, still so sedately that Miss
Armory's keenest instincts failed her.

" Have you said all you can think of?" she
asked, pleasantly.

" Oh, no," he answered. " I mean to talk a
great deal to you yet. My *wait* ought to show
you that."

Miss Armory felt a new degree of exhilaration.

"Very well," she answered. "But don't forget my offer of friendliness.

"No," he said, "I am not likely to. Good-bye, Miss Armory, and thank you. Prudence tells me she is going to the theatre with you to-night."

"Yes; good-bye, or rather *au revoir*."

He took her hand again with the same stiff formality, and was gone in a moment, leaving Miss Armory a brilliant figure in the centre of the beautiful room, but he carried away the very vaguest impression of her personal charms. Something about her, indeed, had made talking to her agreeable, independent of his desire to hear her opinions; but he never analyzed effects upon himself. Indeed, it was not in the nature of the man to take his own feelings into account. A few ambitions he possessed, a few set ideas. A certain plan of life he had devised as being philosophically and ideally the best, but he could contrive to work toward that end without the relaxation of Miss Armory's brilliant smiles or epigrammatic conversation. She was a type, he told himself, entirely outside of his life. He needed her as little as he needed the æstheticism of the London in which he found himself and Prudence.

When he left Cornwall Gardens he wandered rather aimlessly about, unconsciously seeking a

certain physical repose upon one of the benches
in Hyde Park. It was a wintry day, yet the sun,
being still high in the heavens, pierced the fog
with something like illumination. Fielding sat
still in the half-mist, thinking intently, and indulg-
ing in those plans for the future which occupied
half his waking thoughts. Yet even as that visionary to-morrow framed itself in genial colors,
bringing a look of unutterable joy to the man's
clear-cut, strong face, he reverted to his recent talk
with Miss Armory, and a new channel, less vigor-
ous and hopeful, was given to his thoughts.

He had started out that morning believing he
should find just the assistance he needed in Miss
Armory; but he was compelled to own himself
disappointed. What was it he had asked of her?
Something he now believed she could not understand; yet how well she had talked! How readily she had found answers to his meagre words!
He could not tell how to frame his complaint
against the brilliant, good-humored young lady,
yet he knew that he had reason to be disheart-
ened. As he found the benches of the Park on
so cold a morning peculiarly unresponsive, he got
up, and, stretching his limbs, walked away in the
direction of Piccadilly; but as he went he owned
to himself that he was depressed in the extreme.
He sauntered on, still idling both in his gait and
train of thought, but, as he walked, the characters

of a certain advertisement grew luminous before his eyes—

"CHRIST LEAVING THE PRÆTORIUM."

I think he had encountered the words a dozen times before he found himself in Bond Street, mechanically directing his steps toward the Doré Gallery. He paid his shilling, stopped to look at a gorgeous book on sale, and then going into the very glaring little gallery, experienced a certain shock on seeing Prudence and Mrs. Crane seated on one of the circular benches.

VII.

MRS. CRANE wore her most absorbed air. She was looking at the large mass of color representing that most pathetic, marvellous moment in the life of Christ. Prudence was also studying the picture, but with the air of one ready to dimple into smiles at anything more interesting and attractively personal.

"Oh, Jonas!" said Mrs. Crane, brightly, as she extended a cordial hand. Prudence looked delighted, and made room for Jonas at her side.

"Now," said Mrs. Crane, "this is just what a clergyman ought to like, and *isn't* it wonderful? Just look at those Jewish women, and those children! That dear little thing there — *isn't* it perfect?"

Jonas looked. "There is a great deal of color," he said, critically.

"Oh, but you know," said Mrs. Crane, "that's what they *like* so over here now. Don't you remark it? They make color a perfect—a perfect idol."

Jonas, whose eyes had unconsciously been filled with the tender harmonies in Cornwall Gardens, answered nothing for a moment. Then he said, studying the picture,

"Well, it isn't my idea of the scene." And he turned to Miss Marlitt. "Prue looks very tired," he said, smiling.

"Oh, no wonder," said Mrs. Crane. "She's going to be such a belle! She's bewildered with invitations and attentions, and now Lady Frances Holbrook wants us to go to her manor-house in the country. Really, I had *no* idea, until I came over, the English were *so* cordial."

"They're perfectly lovely," said Prudence. "Don't you want to come and have some lunch with us? If I look tired, so do you. Come, Aunt Rebecca, do remember all there is to be done before this evening."

Mrs. Crane stood up with a pleased sort of importance. "Yes," she said, looking at Jonas for approbation, "Prudence is regularly in society."

Prue laughed. It was her old gay laugh, yet her eyes sought those of Jonas with a furtive air.

"Aren't you proud of me, Jonas?" she said, coaxingly.

"Of course," he answered, gravely; "but I wish you looked less tired."

He stood up and followed the ladies down-stairs, where they took a cab, and Jonas, sitting opposite to Mrs. Crane, listened to her discourse upon London society, now and then glancing at Prue's fair face to read in it some expression of sympathy with his distrust. But there was none. The girl was supremely contented, supremely happy. She ate her luncheon, and talked about the afternoon, freely imparting her plans to Jonas, displaying a little note-book full of engagements, and wondering whether she should enjoy the theatre. Mrs. Crane touched Jonas's arm with a significant smile.

"Of course she will," she said, radiantly. "*We* know who'll be there. That young Mr. Simmonson. Did you know, Jonas, his uncle is a real lord over here, and one day he is to have the title."

"I knew," said Jonas.

"*Well*," said Mrs. Crane, drawing a long breath, "I think if *some* people in Ponkamak would hear of our doings, they *would* be surprised."

"I am writing home to-night," said Jonas, a little grimly. "What shall I say?"

"Oh, what you like. Tell them about Prudence's success here."

It was the second time he had heard the word applied to the girl whom he fain would shelter from the world with his very life, but coming from Mrs. Crane it had a bolder significance.

"How am I to say that, Prue?" he said, smiling across the table upon Prue's contented young face.

"Oh," said the girl, gayly, "call it fun — that's what it is. Tell them I'm having a perfectly elegant time."

"I am writing to George Maybery," said Jonas, "and I won't forget your message."

In spite of their many obligations, the ladies declared after luncheon they had an hour or two on their hands, and would like Jonas to take them to see something. He was eager enough for their service, and standing in Regent Street hurriedly enumerated such places as he considered likely to interest them. Westminster occurred to them all as peculiarly congenial. The Abbey was one of the spots which Jonas had frequently discussed with Prudence in a remote way, aided by stereoscopic views and a magazine article or two they read together during the winter evenings. It hurt him a little to see that the calm radiance of her face remained unchanged while he made his suggestion, and when they were in a cab whirling toward the Abbey, she said, with her lovely smile, "Westminster, isn't it?" And almost before Jonas answered "Yes," she had turned to ask some trivial question of her aunt.

But in the Abbey Prudence's fluttering thoughts concentrated — solemnified by the silent, hidden presences to which Jonas conducted her reverently, wishing he could lift his face up to the very vault of heaven, with bared head, as he stood among them. Prue looked, asked questions, and listened to Jonas with respectful attention; but what would he not have given for an hour of the old sweet companionship, in which the girl gave freely all that she had to give, while he unlocked the storehouse of his mind, or lavished on her the homage of his deep, whole-souled nature? That there had been no promise for the future exchanged between them had only seemed to strengthen his devotion and her trustful dependence. She knew—she must have known—he was only waiting to speak until she was older, in obedience to a promise made her dead brother. Six months ago he and Prudence would have stood in this grand old monastery with but one feeling, and now the girl was listening and looking because she knew it was a part of her education, and it would be silly to forget the names and the tombs, and Jonas's descriptions were more interesting than the guide-book, or even a verger. As for Jonas, he steeled himself bravely to the subtle change in their relationship, and went on, elaborating, if possible, more than he would have done had his heart beat less sadly. Mrs. Crane was brilliant, alert, and smilingly sarcastic in her remarks. She meant to write home very well and solemnly on the subject, but the Abbey, like all else that was English, afforded her a certain amount of amusement. Of late she was rarely in a mood to be impressed, and she moved about among the monuments seeking some object for her brilliant sarcasm. That tomb holding the mortal remains of the man who moved

nations to tears or laughter held her quiet, and
subdued her most eager remarks; but she said in a
moment that he had belonged to all the world, and
moved away with a look on her face in which there
was, singular to say, no thought of self. They had
wandered about the cloisters, looked at the close
in the pale, foggy light, and examined with some
interest the low door-ways leading to the various
clerical residences of the Abbey. The afternoon
service began, and, as the organ pealed forth, the
American party decided to take their places among
the worshippers, interested to observe the entrance
of the choristers and listen to the sweet, passion-
less music of the cathedral choir.

Jonas was glad of the quiet. He sat in one of
the old stalls, looking now and then at Prudence's
beautiful face shining beneath the broad-brimmed
felt hat. The girl's rich tints filled him with a sort
of peace: he hardly knew what to call it — what
name to give the love and longing that sometimes
crept into his very soul. Was it, he wondered, because she was so unutterably lovely? He looked
intently at the soft cheek, the lashes which curled
upon it, half shading the dark sweetness of her
eyes — at the waves of warmly colored hair that
showed beneath her hat—at the delicately moulded chin, the child-like bloom of the lips—he looked
at her, I say, feasting his eyes, his very soul, upon
her beauty. Yet he was almost unaware that he

6

was counting up her charms, that he was rejoic-
ing in her exceeding loveliness; something higher,
stronger, sweeter, was in the conscious part of his
mind — the dream that had filled him since boy-
hood, the hope that had made of toil a pleasure.
He leaned his face down upon his hand, and passionately conjured up the vision that had been the
day-dream of all those working, toiling years. It
was Prudence, always Prudence, the girl sheltered
in his keeping, the wife waiting for his coming, the
mother caring for his children, the woman who was
to be the inspiration, the guardian, the friend of
all his life! And had this been reality, or only the
fantastic folly of a man who passionately idealizes
not only his chances of life, but the object of his
concentrated desires? Jonas, unnerved, unstrung,
by all the mental conflicts of the past few days, refused to answer to himself these unrestful questions.   He tried to reduce thought to mere numb-
ness, if it would not flow into another channel, and
Prudence, glancing shyly toward him, was struck
with the repressed intensity of the man's face and
look.   To her vision, Jonas, dear old Jonas, sat
there a tall, strong figure, with the same plain, earnest face she always remembered, and had never
criticised. She never questioned whence came the
light that filled his eyes when he was preaching, or,
perhaps, when he was walking up and down the
old-fashioned parlor in Ponkamak, talking to her

or reading aloud. Those hidden chambers of the mind, those untrodden, mysterious places, which were Self in the man, she had never considered. Their outcome she felt without analyzing the source, or questioning whether there might not be a tremulous fascination in response to the movements of his inner being. She looked up at him now, realizing the lines of fatigue about the honest eyes and strong mouth, seeing with swift regret that he was pale and tired; but no depths were stirred, no longing to know the meaning of the change in his familiar face. She would have slipped one of her little hands tenderly toward him had she dared; she would have gladly ministered to his physical needs; indeed, she began to wonder whether she had been right in urging Jonas to stay in London when he had found them on his way to Nice; but her introspection went no farther than this vague doubt of her own infallibility, and compassion for the weariness expressed in Jonas's face.

"It is over," he said, in a moment, while Prudence was thinking what she ought to do.

Prudence started, and demurely walked after her aunt and Jonas down the aisle, a little flattered by the glances of admiration freely lavished upon her as she went. She forgot to say anything to Jonas about his health as he put her, with Mrs. Crane, into a cab; but then, as she remembered

later, she should see him the next day. When
they had driven off, the young man started for another solitary walk. Where his steps took him
that afternoon Jonas Fielding never knew. He
walked on and on, piercing the fog, through which
street venders with their flaring lamps were to be
seen, before he found himself at his hotel; and,
after so much incoherent reflection, it was somewhat of a relief to find some home letters, and also
a little note from Miss Armory. The latter was
quickly read, but Jonas held it a long time in his
hands. It bore the air of Belgravia in its faint
scent, pretty monogram, and unobtrusive crest.

"DEAR MR. FIELDING" (it ran),—"I really feel
that we have made a good beginning to-day, but
came to no ending. You must come up soon
again, and may be sure of finding me at home between eleven and one o'clock any morning. The
chief object of this note, however, is to ask you to
try and look in at the Lyceum this evening, where
you will find us in box No. —. Don't think I am
going to be too persistent in my efforts to control
destiny. I only want you to see that I am not the
ruling power you seemed to imagine. Do you
know, I felt, after you went away, as though I
would give a great deal—for—well, even the cob-
ble-stones on Broadway. Sincerely yours,
"HELENA LISLE ARMORY."

Jonas re-read the letter once or twice before he replaced it in its envelope.   He smiled to himself with the air of a man who wishes he could alter a decided opinion.   Then, after one or two turns about his room, he sat down and penned the following reply:

"MY DEAR MISS ARMORY,—I am very much obliged to you for your kindness in writing me that note, and I am glad that anything I have said made you feel as if you would like to see your native land soon again.   We shall have many more talks if you are always as kind as you were to-day. I feel very much unhinged lately, but I don't know as anything in particular has happened to unhinge me, only I suppose we must have periods of peculiar mental and moral shock once in so often.   I would rather have had just this one in America, I think.   I am not in the humor for the theatre to-night, or I should certainly go, but I hope your party will enjoy it very much.   Very truly yours,

"JONAS P. FIELDING."

When he had written this note the young man held it a long time purposelessly in his hands. Then he went down-stairs, and with a sedate politeness asked to have it posted at once.

VIII.

THERE is an old house not far from the Strand in which Mr. Barley Simmonson has his studio. How that popular young man had come to set up his artistic gods in such a sombre neighborhood was a question of wonder until his friends learned to know the house; then surprise merged into something like envy, for nowhere in London could there have been more beautiful rooms. A great many people know the old house now. It is in a quiet street full of sanctuaries, and there is a vague charm, half of antiquity, half of splendid solemnity, about the vistas on every side. The house once belonged to a famous duke, whose coat of arms is still above the mantels, and in faded colors painted on the wall. Few outward changes have been made since the pompous day of his Grace — the old knocker, the link-boys' extinguishers, the heavy door, the porter's niche, remain in solemn preservation, and the dusky hall-way and staircases are ponderous with suggestions of the past.

Mr. Simmonson had two brilliant rooms upstairs, in which royalty had danced many a gay measure a hundred years ago. The lower windows

look out upon an old bit of London, and catch the
rushing of the river, with its suggestions of many
a century's ebb and flow; at the side the windows
front a peaceful, old-fashioned garden, such as one
sees in the very heart of London—fragrant and
green, even in winter-time. Within, everything
that a really good instinct for color and arrange-
ment could do he had done for the room. I cannot hope to describe the means employed for this
wonderfully harmonious end. Miss Armory used
to say that if at times she forgot that she was in
a real workshop, she always remembered that she
was among the most beautiful fabrics, the most artistic furnishings, softened, harmonized, by the di-
vinest tints time can devise or money buy. Simmonson's piano stood in a darkly polished space
near the embrasure of those windows looking out
upon the river, and the window-seats covered in
faded red velvet had panes of stained glass here
and there, so that his listeners sitting there looked
often like saints in a shrine, aureole-crowned, vibrating with some mysterious light—at least Helena thought of this on the days when Prudence visited the studio, and the girl sat for her picture in a
desultory sort of fashion, interrupted by the fitful-
ness of the painter's mood or Prudence's declara-
tion that she was tired.

It was a fascinating sort of occupation, I think,
for all the party: a few weeks which drifted into

their lives unexpectedly, but bringing a charm
which no one thought of analyzing any more than
they wondered who had first owned the faded
mediæval splendors of Barley Simmonson's room.
Mrs. Boyce used to bring her work, but Helena never made even a feint of thus occupying
her fingers. She moved about the room from
time to time, played bits of music, exchanged sen-
timents and feelings with Barley Simmonson, and
freely vented her admiration of little Prudence,
who sat in a shining space, wearing her satin gown,
and holding some fading yellow roses in her hands.

Those were whole hours of life, Miss Armory
sometimes said, yet she believed in them as con-
tributions to the warmer needs of nature and feeling. She would not have sacrificed her share in
them for any consideration, and her mind was only
disturbed when she thought of Jonas Fielding, and
forced herself to believe that Barley Simmonson
intended to let himself fall in love.

Moving his eyes from the canvas to Prue's face
above the creamy satin and careless lace, it was
not possible that he should not be at least moved
to sentiment; but Miss Armory had seen the
man's intention that night at the Lyceum Theatre. It was not only that he had brought, as an
offering to Prudence, a tall white lily, which the
girl had some difficulty in holding or " bearing "
throughout the play, but that since the talk of

the morning Helena's instincts were all sharpened
where Prudence was concerned. A flavor of Puritanism clung about Helena in the midst of her
later surroundings. She could not shake off her
keen sense of justice, and it now smote her conscience that she had not frankly warned Jonas of
what she felt to be in the air. But of what nature
was his and Prudence's relationship? Helena had
gathered enough to know that the man loved Prudence passionately, and that he believed in her
loyalty to him. No engagement existed between
them founded on word; yet the very nature of a
bond that has for its security what must remain
unspoken appealed to Helena's best instincts. The
fine appreciation of the girl covered with clear vision and unwavering opinion what might have been
debatable ground in a mind like Prue's. Miss Armory told herself that she would have been faith-
ful forever on such an understanding, and it would
be double treason to desert a post to which your
unformulated sense of honor alone held you. In
this fashion Miss Armory reasoned during the first
fortnight of the sittings, seeing Jonas Fielding only
twice in the interval, for he had unexpectedly gone
out of town. That he looked to Miss Armory for
some sympathy had been evident to her in the
note he wrote in starting. "I am off," he said,
"to preach for a friend at N——, and I regret not
having seen you when I called yesterday, for I

should like to have taken counsel with you as to how to address the middle classes who will hear me ; not that I do not feel strongly with the 'multitude,' but that I am all at sea as to English instincts. I should not have demanded any theology of you, you may be sure, for I know your lack of even a religious impression. Perhaps, while you were instructing me in the traditions of the people, I should have shown you the error of your way. At all events, I believe we should have done each other good. I shall be at Simmonson's next Thursday."

Miss Armory thought she had never received a note she liked so well, and, in spite of her mental uneasiness, she waited with some impatience for Fielding's appearance on the Thursday. In the midst of a sword-thrust, even, we may care for the hand that holds the weapon, and to Miss Armory there was already a fascination in Jonas Fielding's disapproval.

"You are working very badly," she said to the painter about three o'clock that afternoon.

Simmonson threw down his brush, gazing sadly upon Prudence.

"Am I?" he said. "Yes, I suppose so." And then the heavy curtains were moved, and Jonas Fielding was announced. Helena gave a start. He shook hands with Mr. Simmonson, who seemed glad of an absolute excuse for idleness.

"It is getting too dark for work," he said, standing up; and Prudence moved with evident gratification at the change.

"Now, Miss Marlitt," said Simmonson, in a moment, "I will show you those costumes you wanted to see."

The two moved away, followed by Mrs. Boyce, and Helena found herself apart with Fielding.

"How did the sermon go?" she said, pleasantly.

"Well enough. I found out that the simplest way was to appeal to common human nature." His eyes wandered toward Prudence, who was sitting in the window with her lap full of color.

"And the sittings?" he said, with a smile.

"Very well. I wish you had been here. I think you would have enjoyed them."

"Which means I should have had my prejudices removed?"

"Oh no; I have been saving something special for that."

Helena's dark eyes flashed merrily.

"What?—do let me work myself up to it properly."

"The private view at the Grosvenor—it will be to-morrow. I felt that to be my *pièce de résistance*."

"Well," said Jonas, "I won't ask any questions. If you are kind enough to invite me, I shall go as ignorantly as any juryman could begin a case; but —will you accept my verdict?"

Helena's expression changed.

"Oh," said Jonas, laughing; "I don't mean as an influence upon your own thought—don't imagine I am quite so self-confident; but I mean, will you believe in the sincerity of my own beliefs after this supreme test?"

Helena paused.

"Do you know anything of art?" she said, in a moment. They were sitting in one of the windows, Helena leaning back against the side, Jonas on a low chair near by. He swept the room slowly with his gaze, and then brought his eyes back to Miss Armory's charming figure.

"No," he said, conclusively.

"Well," said the young lady, "what can I do tomorrow, then?—my object being to show you the real art in æstheticism, and that in it could be true feeling, real action."

"Even though you scorned it so forcibly to me the other day?"

"I scorned its exaggerations. I scorn them yet. Come, Mr. Fielding, be fair, and wide-minded. Accept, with tolerance of others' needs, what you do not need yourself."

They had been using a light tone of banter, but now into the man's face came a look which startled Helena as she watched him: it brought out painfully the haggard lines about his mouth and eyes.

"I am trying to do that very thing," he said, quietly. "I am afraid I never thought of it until lately."

Mrs. Boyce interrupted them at this moment. She too had some questions to ask about the country sermon. Meanwhile Barley Simmonson was heard idling at the piano.

"So you've been preaching to the people, Fielding, have you?" he said, smiling, and lingering over a soft cadence.

"Who are the people?" asked Jonas, with his shrewd smile. "I've been trying to find out ever since I came here — for, from what I am told, it seems to me my lot in life, were I an Englishman, would be among them. You will be a lord, I suppose, one day, Mr. Simmonson, and if I were to be an Englishman, I should probably have to consort with your grocer, and you couldn't know me."

Simmonson looked deeply interested, but he said nothing for a moment. He did not so much scorn his prospective rank as that he said its obligations hampered him. He sat silently a moment, his Greek head bent backward slightly, his eyes half closed.

"*Noblesse oblige*," he murmured, with soft disdain. He was playing vagrant bars of Schubert. "When we can realize the poet's meaning" (a sad arpeggio) "of a higher life; when existence grows fuller; when sensations deepen; when the soul

grows conscious of the infinite, which pierces or
vibrates through the finite; when song" (and here
Barley's eyes grew illumined)—"when song is but
the outcome of nature; when nature fuses itself
with the illimitable; when Passion finds its final
utterance, and our moments—our moments throb
with the actual in what we call Emotion and Life"
(Barley's finger touched one note over and over in
the treble with a sad insistence)—"then even *rank*
may have its measure of intensity: then we may
say 'my lord,' meaning 'my gentle'" (Barley's
smile was very sweet—he looked at every one);
"then we may wear laurel in Westminster; then
we may assemble as one palpitating, perfect Soul."

"Well," said Mrs. Boyce, leaning over one end
of the grand piano, "that sounds very well, Mr.
Simmonson. I hope we shall all live to see something of this Arcadia in the House of Lords."

Helena slowly turned her eyes upon the artist,
who continued to strike desultory notes, and look
with a cold, sad smile upon the little company.

"I wonder how much of it you'll repeat heartily
ten years hence?" Miss Armory said, and almost
instantly colored, for she observed Jonas smiling
approval, with a half-triumphant, half-mischievous
"I told you so" in his expression. Therefore she
felt it her duty to add, in a low tone, which he
only heard—"I understand what you mean. I
maintain that the false ground in æstheticism is

only in the establishing a standard of *feeling.*
Now I am sure I can explain myself better at
the Grosvenor. You will come?"

"Of course," said Jonas. And while they briefly
arranged for the hour and place, Mrs. Boyce carried Prudence into the inner room to make her
driving toilet; and then Helena moved away, list-
lessly turning over some draperies, while Fielding
sat regarding the artist with a gaze that became
entirely compassionate. The room was very still,
yet to Helena it seemed, a few minutes later, to
vibrate with feeling that might have been sound;
for Prudence returned, and one of those silent
moments, full of action and significance, occurred.
Simmonson sat leaning his arms on the music-
stand, his eyes seeking Miss Marlitt's; Fielding
also regarded the girl critically, and under this
double gaze an air of shyness or coquetry took
possession of her.

She blushed faintly, and absorbed herself in but-
toning a refractory glove. Fielding and Helena
moved forward together to offer assistance, and
Prue, with a little sigh, held out her slim wrist in-
differently to either. It was a moment of confusion in Helena's mind. She never knew how, in
putting her own warm, soft fingers down to the
little wrist, they touched those of Fielding, and by
some awkward accident were a moment held in
his. The unexpected contact startled him, but he

looked swiftly at Prudence. Helena for the first
time in her life felt the warm blood tingling in her
fingers, and rushing, as it were, to her heart and
cheeks. She kept her face passionately down-bent
during one of those vibrating eternal moments by
which we are told mortals should count time. It
seemed to Helena at last that she must move or
speak; but Prudence, whose glove was now comfortably arranged, came to her relief with her clear
little contented treble.

"Thank you, dear," she said, and prettily kissed
Miss Armory's pink cheek.

The confusion was over. Helena felt that she
could meet Fielding's eyes, and trust to the sound
of her own voice, but the leaving was all confused
in her memory. As they went down the dusky
staircases she was faintly conscious that Mr. Simmonson was saying to Prudence, impressively—

"Then I may call to-morrow morning—you will
be sure to see me?"

They were like words heard in a dream. All
that seemed real to Helena was a sense of folly
if not weak-mindedness; but a whole lifetime may
depend upon five moments; and, as they drove
home, Miss Armory was conscious of having made
a plunge into the future.

IX.

FIELDING awoke the next morning with a defined consciousness that the day was to mean something for him. He had spent the evening previous in Guildford Street, and while Prudence was absent a few moments from the room, Mrs. Crane had discoursed brilliantly upon their social position. She had been writing a great many letters home. To her own family she had suggested the possibility of Prudence's "wearing a title."

"But I thought," said Fielding, in mild protest —"I thought you objected to the aristocracy."

Mrs. Crane was momentarily confused; but then such perplexities with her always wore the air of an effort to be strictly lenient in her judgment of her companion.

"Well," she said, slowly, "if Prudence marries here, I prefer it should be the best. I think Mr. Simmonson will speak very soon to her. In fact, Jonas, I don't mind telling you, as an old friend of the family, he has consulted me already."

Jonas had found no words to answer this, and just then Prudence returned, wearing, with an air of brilliant coquetry, a new gown, which she called

7

upon Jonas to admire. She had had it made for the Grosvenor private view.

"Mr. Simmonson designed it," she explained— "or, I should say, he and Miss Armory between them."

Jonas felt a sudden thrill of disgust. It was to him as if they were dressing her up for an exhibition of her charms to the vulgar, gaping admiration of a crowd. But the gown, he admitted, was charming. It was a serge of a curious shade of red, warm in tone, and yet sombre; the sleeves were puffed, but altogether it had a touch of almost Puritanical simplicity about it. The rich curves of the girl's figure showed to perfection in it, and Jonas thought he had never seen her face lovelier than it looked above the lustrous red and the narrow frill of lace. With this gown was to be worn a bonnet with plumes, and short wide strings of satin the color of her gown. Prudence arranged herself gleefully, and was pleased by Jonas's approbation. When he was leaving, she followed him out into the hall, Mrs. Crane being absorbed by some important letters received by the last post.

"Dear Jonas," the girl said, looking up at him with one of her old sweet glances, "you seem troubled—what is it?"

"Not troubled, Prue," the young man answered, searching the depths of her eyes half sadly; "but I think I may have been foolish lately. Tell me, are you ready to have me come to you to-morrow evening, and tell you all that I have to say?"

"Oh, Jonas!" she answered, eagerly, "do! I shall be *so* glad!" and she held her hand out for a gentle, affectionate good-bye.

Prudence and Mrs. Crane were to go to the Grosvenor with Mrs. Boyce's party, and it was agreed between Miss Armory and Jonas that he should meet them at the gallery. Accordingly, about three o'clock, he started for Bond Street through the fog, thinking much more of the human than the pictured presences awaiting him. He was somewhat confused by the animation in the entrance to the Grosvenor. English "private views" were completely unfamiliar to him, and the presence of aristocracy, fashion, art, and science rather bewildered him. He was conscious, as he went toward the staircase, of Mrs. Poynsett's tired, friendly smile; of Hergliebe's dark head and broad shoulders; of the agreeable Lady Ericson, to whom Miss Armory had introduced him; and, indeed, of nearly all the faces he had known in London the past five weeks. Then he found himself following some ladies in curious garments up the staircases and into the group of rooms. There, for a moment, all seemed confusion. The walls were assuredly richly hung, but Fielding's eyes took in only a sense of many colors. The moving figures were as diverse and as peculiar as if half a dozen centuries had contributed to the fashions of one single hour; and Jonas stood still, in a side door-way, searching among the quaintly dressed women for the figures and faces that he knew.

It so chanced that at that moment Miss Armory had disengaged herself from her party, and was standing before one of Albert Moore's pictures. Fielding's eye caught sight of her figure speedily. She was curiously dressed, and the young man looked a moment at her gown of dull-colored velvet with trimmings of rich brown fur—the large bonnet of felt, in color like her gown, which framed her face luxuriantly, if possible adding a new softness to her calm, patrician beauty. For a moment Jonas enjoyed the impression of womanly elegance and grace which she conveyed without feeling any impulse to move even in so attractive a direction, but before she had left the picture he was at her side. It was only when she turned her eyes toward him, and held out her hand, that some vague fluttering remembrance of the touch of her fingers yesterday crossed his mind; but he looked at her with kindly eagerness, trying to dissipate the idea quickly.

"You are punctual," she said, smiling; and Fielding remarked that she looked brilliant, but with the unnatural brilliancy which sometimes succeeds long waking hours.

"I like to be punctual in all things," he said, answering her smile. "And yet, do you know, Miss Armory, I stayed awake last night discovering that I have been a most lamentable dawdler."

Miss Armory continued to look pleasantly at him without speaking.

"Now, I suppose," Fielding said, "it won't do to chain you to a conversation. I must find Prudence, and then will you show me the pictures?"

He laughed, and Helena was struck with the almost boyish radiance of his face. He looked like a man who had been performing or contemplating some greatly benevolent action, and he had such a large cheerfulness about him that it seemed to the girl only to intensify the depression of her own mood.

"Prue is in there," she said, indicating the next room. "Do you see the little court about her, Mr. Fielding? She is looking perfectly lovely. She is the *furor* of this most critical occasion."

Fielding's benevolent demeanor continued. "Ah," he said, "of course she is lovely! of course they would all see it. I feel much more generous lately. Perhaps I had better not interrupt her just now." The memory of last night's good-bye was still in his mind, the feeling of Prue's little hand clung to his fingers, the light of her sweet, uplifted eyes seemed to be the radiance that fell everywhere about him.

"Suppose we talk a little first," he said, "if

I may take up a quarter of an hour of your time."

Helena assented, and they wound along silently regarding the pictures.

Since yesterday it seemed to Helena that every purpose was changed. She had no longer that alert desire to make Fielding see things as she viewed them. During the long hours of the night she had grown conscious of many conflicting feelings; and while a sudden passionate distrust of herself, her judgments of life, her basis of philosophic thought, had tormented her, yet her duty toward Jonas Fielding was always luminously distinct. She had a fixed purpose in her mind, yet she found it difficult to put it into words.

I think all her life Helena will remember just that moment with the sharp distinctness our passionate, our weak, or our saddening memories have. There is a picture of Mr. Whistler's always connected with it. If she owned it, and saw it hourly on her wall, she could not more clearly know its misty, ineffable tenderness of gray and green and blue. She stood still with Jonas a moment, apparently studying the picture intently, and then, with a great effort, she turned and said, gravely,

"Do you remember my 'Wait?'"

He looked at her brightly. "Yes—yes, indeed."

"It is done with," she said, smiling faintly. "I have something special to say to you. Do not

"I THINK YOU ARE A MAN TO WHOM ONE CAN SPEAK
FEARLESSLY."

wait.   I think you are a man to whom one can
speak fearlessly.   Well, then, Mr. Fielding, if you
care for anything in life, stretch out your hand and
try to take it at once to yourself."

The radiance of Fielding's face was undimmed,
but it grew thoughtful.

" I know what you mean," he said, in a low tone,
"and I shall answer you fairly.   I love Prudence,
and she loves me ; we both have known it for years ;
but long ago I promised Marlitt not to bind her to
any engagement until she was twenty-one.   The
time had passed two months ago, and I came here,
as you know, on my way to Nice.   For a week or
two the fitting moment did not come, and then I
experienced the shock, you know, of finding her in
such strange surroundings.   So I said nothing.   I
was wrong ; but—   Yes, your ' Wait ' did seem to
me impressive, or perhaps it urged on my own
thought, but it is all right now.   My doubts are
gone," he said, with the smile Helena had learned
to watch for curving his lips.   "They are gone.
To-morrow, or to-day, it shall be settled between
us ; but thank you, thank you—you have been *so*
good."

Miss Armory was silent for a moment ; then she
said, in a low, tired voice, " Why did he ask you to
wait ?"

" Marlitt ?   Oh," said Jonas, skimming the past,
as it were, with the lightness of one who sees an

old error of judgment vanishing—"he wished Prudence to be admired in a more general way, to see the world a little. My life is to be an active one in Boston, but a hard one in many ways. I am not rich, and my wife must share the simplicity as well as the purposes of my calling. Prudence, Marlitt said, ought to see the other side; and she *has* seen it," he said, joyously. "Even Marlitt would be satisfied now; but, Miss Armory, it has been the one passion, the one thought, the one purpose of my life, apart from my actual duties. I did not know, I was not sure, at least until yesterday, how all ends had been tending toward this result. Life will begin now."

Helena was still motionless, with an effort to keep even the faintest shadow of her feeling from her eyes, which were resting softly on his strong, clear face.

"You must make things clear, *perfectly* clear," she said, earnestly. "Do not leave any part of your bond now indefinite. Is there anything I can do or say—I mean to give you the opportunity for your talk alone with Prudence? Come to Cornwall Gardens, if you like, to-morrow at eleven—she will be there. Let me do that for you."

Jonas hesitated a moment, and then the remembrance of Mrs. Crane's ambitious murmurs last night crossed his mind, and he realized that she might be an obstacle to free speech with Prudence.

"Oh, thank you!" he said, with a happy light in his eyes. "We know—Prue and I—just the one word needed between us to give me the right to call her my own. Then I will go to you to-morrow, Miss Armory."

"It will be all right," she answered, with a sweet, grave smile. Fielding looked at her, conscious of the influence of her womanly sympathy, and moved to make any demand upon it which his impulse suggested. "I hope you know," he said, earnestly, "that if it were for her good I would resign all thought of her; but I cannot believe that. I have cherished her since she could walk, or think, or feel. She learned to read sitting on my knee, with her head against my shoulder. She brought me every grief and every joy. Oh," he said, radiantly, "it could not be."

Helena listened, with every token of interest possible, in silence. Neither spoke for an instant, and then she said, gently, "Oh, I wish you godspeed: she is yours by right."

They turned to look at the pictures, and Helena felt surprised at her own listlessness in leading him into the region of the "æsthetes." Singularly enough, all such interest, where he was concerned, had vanished. She moved about, picking out peculiarities and points to admire or contemplate; but it was with an evident effort. She was eagerly sought for by so many people that Fielding good-humoredly withdrew while she was talking to young Grierson, and, making his way into the next room, he looked about for Prudence.

As Helena had said, the girl had her little court, and she was unquestionably a source of interest and comment to every one in the room. People passed and repassed, looking at the girl's wondrous beauty, half shaded by the bonnet Fielding had seen last night, and he was sufficiently exultant not to notice the expression of complete self-satisfaction which had crept of late into her face. In fact, this period, emphasized by such novel occasions, was one of intense enjoyment to little Prue. She had known for years that she was the prettiest girl in Ponkamak, but the homage paid her there had a dull flavor which made it uninteresting; moreover, it was different from that rendered in London in that it was accompanied by nothing splendid. If she were the prettiest girl in Ponkamak, it was in sober-colored, ugly parlors, among simply dressed women, who loaned each other paper patterns, and thought a black silk good enough for any occasion; but here, on such a day as this, for instance, to be admired in such a magnificent company was enough to stir any girl's pulses — and Prudence was not proof against such homage. She sat on one of the benches with her little court, in which Mr. Simmonson was the favored courtier, feeling a rush of happy color to her cheeks, a thrill of something

"MR. FIELDING, WHAT DO YOU THINK OF THESE PICTURES? THIS IS ART."

which made her almost hope she should never see
Ponkamak any more. She had no adaptability;
she had little or no power of even imitating what
she saw, and certainly no perceptions delicate
enough to appreciate the *raison d'être* even of a
social form or feeling which was entirely new; but
the novelty of her present position amused and interested her, and, in proportion to her lack of per-
ception as to cause and effect, she accepted everything offered as triumphantly personal. She was
glad that Jonas Fielding should see how polite people were to her, and, as he approached, the sweetness of her eyes gave him a welcome.

Mr. Simmonson, who was in close attendance,
looked around at Fielding with a careless greet-
ing.

"Well, Jonas — Mr. Fielding," said Prudence,
with a little, eager, fluttering manner that it was
difficult to define as either animation or nervous
enjoyment — "well, Mr. Fielding, what do you
think of these pictures? This is *Art*."

Prudence pronounced the word with a rapid,
veiled glance at Mr. Simmonson. That young
man evidently had no idea of contributing any but
the complimentary faculty within him to Prudence.
Mediocre as his genius might be, he rendered it
the tribute of silence before such minds as this
young girl's.

"Why," said Jonas, smiling, "I've only looked

about a very little, but Miss Armory has been trying to lead me upward."

"Miss Armory knows what she is talking about,"
said Mr. Simmonson; "she has genuine feeling,
and she is so clever!"

"Oh, isn't she?" said Prudence; "and she says
such funny things. I asked her once how I ought
to talk to an artist, and she gave me one of her
funny little looks, and said, 'Have you any definite opinion about Prussian blue, and—and—'"
Prudence hesitated with her bewitching air.

"Asphaltum?" suggested Simmonson.

"That was it!" cried Prudence, gayly. "I knew
it had something to do with the pavements at
home. Well, she said, if I couldn't make up my
mind about that, I must try and understand yellow ochre, and that was all I could get out of her.
She would only laugh and tease me when I told
her I really meant it."

"But surely," said Fielding, when they had all
done laughing, "Mr. Simmonson must have enlightened you. Come, I really expect an opinion
of some sort from you now."

"But Miss Marlitt objects to first principles,"
said Simmonson, lazily, and evidently wishing art
could be left out of the question. "She won't admit anything but a literary quality in a picture."

"I like a nice little story in a picture," said Prue,
gayly. "I have been telling Mr. Simmonson if all

this is *real* art, then I'll never buy anything but a chromo. I like a picture one can make up a long story about."

Simmonson, who looked ineffably dreamy and willowy leaning against the velvet bench, was conscious of a very matter-of-fact, reasonable moment.

"And therefore," he said, "you give the painter, as a workman, credit for nothing at all. Any penny-a-liner might do his work for him; his art means nothing."

Prudence stared.

"What do you mean?" she said, audaciously; and then, glancing in the direction of Simmonson's waving fingers, she added, "Oh, *don't*—please don't show me those horrid things over there! Those pictures all look so hungry. I wish so I could give all the poor people Mr. Burne-Jones and those other gentlemen paint a good dinner. They want beef tea. . . . Now, Mr. Simmonson says that is the highest expression of art."

Prudence's cheerful little appeals to Jonas struck Simmonson as the most amusing sort of self-defence; the three people were so utterly asunder in thought and feeling at the moment, that it was impossible to harmonize a single pulsation by the aid of art. Dimly Jonas realized this, because the man's nature was deep enough, his intellect sufficiently piercing, to know that there existed widely untravelled spaces beyond his vision. In some

fashion he realized that this question of art-mean-
ings was not his to decide. He would not pretend
to say how a painter should put on his strokes—
how a painter should illustrate his theme. All
that he felt as sacred to the man's own genius.
As for Simmonson, he was indifferent, only wishing Prudence would allow him to conduct her
about the rooms, and talk to him in amusing gen-
eralities. But to Prudence the moment was one
in which she felt called upon to be critical, and
underlying her air of perplexity was a flavor of
sarcasm which it amused her to see Simmonson
utterly overlooked. She poised her pretty head,
looked at this and that, and laughed a great deal
at nearly everything.

"I can't make out what Mr. Simmonson means,"
she said, finally. "He talks of the pictorial and
the literary quality in a picture. Which was I,
Mr. Simmonson, when you painted me, please?"
And the girl darted a charming but very flippant
look at the artist.

"You were everything," Simmonson said. "Too
much for me to paint. Now come over to see
those Dutch pictures. Don't refuse opportunities
of enlightenment that may never come again."

Prudence eagerly complied; and Jonas, after observing how many people showered attentions upon
her, determined to leave her to undisturbed enjoyment of what he was pleased to call "the hilarity

of the occasion." He said a few words of good-
bye, and then tried to find Miss Armory; but that
young lady was in an animated group, and Jonas
decided to go home, and write a few lines to Prudence which should explain the motive of his visit
to Cornwall Gardens the next day. On the way
out he lingered over some pictures in the last
room, and there he was suddenly conscious of
Miss Armory approaching from the right hand,
with a searching air.

"Oh, you are here!" she said, quickly. "Do you
know I wanted so much to say a little word to you."

Jonas looked pleased.

"I want you to promise," she said, rushing into
the subject, "that you will give me an hour of
your time—some day before you leave London."

"An hour?" said Jonas, with alacrity. "A whole
day, a week—any time."

She looked at him critically. The joy in his
heart still found a reflection in his quiet eyes.

"Well, only don't forget," she said, "which
means, don't be selfishly exclusive."

Jonas might have been more flattered by all this
if something very impersonal, almost chilling, had
not shown itself in the young lady's manner. While
she talked she seemed to regard him, he told himself, simply as an abstract means to some end, and
he was sure that Miss Armory's interests were as
often purely philosophical or intellectual as personal.

X.

MISS ARMORY certainly contrived to make things very simple for Jonas the next day. When he arrived at Cornwall Gardens the butler solemnly showed him up into the same little room which he had visited before; but instead of Helena idling over rich embroideries, Prudence was seated near the fire, motionless, but with eagerly dilated vision.

It is certain that Jonas had arrived there with no thought of Miss Armory beyond the general consciousness of her beneficent genius, yet almost involuntarily there rose to his mind a picture of her effective figure on that previous occasion. Perhaps he had not appreciated the impression she created upon him; perhaps it was that Prue, moving to the window among the æsthetic luxuries of the boudoir, seemed to bear about her a flavor of Ponkamak that nothing could subdue. In either case the young man felt, as he came in, a sensation of disturbed preconceptions. He wished, for a moment, that he had seen Prudence in Guildford Street. There, at least, nothing confused his ideals.

Prudence stood still like a frightened child; and

when she gave Jonas her hand, it was with a look as if she expected a rebuke.

"Prue!" he said—he was longing to take her in his arms, to hold her in his strong embrace; the first, but such as would show her what a life's shelter might be—"Prudence!" he exclaimed, "oh, my darling!"

The girl was trembling visibly. She still stood silently regarding him with a timid, beautiful gaze.

"What is it, dear?" said Jonas. "Don't you know I ought to have come two months ago? The time I agreed to wait was up; but I thought it best first to let you see this—this life here."

"Yes, yes," said Prudence, still fixedly regarding him. "I know—yes, that is just it, Jonas dear," she added, tenderly.

"Just what?" said Jonas, to whom the radiance of belief yet gave a joyous tone and impassioned expression—"just what, dear?"

He held his hands toward her; he made a little movement as though he would take her at once into his strong arms.

"Don't you see?" said Prudence, holding herself aloof from him. "Just as you say, I've seen—seen the world. I don't think"—she looked at him with a sort of wild pleading; Jonas remembered the same look when she was a child asking for a midsummer holiday with him, or for a new doll— "I don't think I'd like to be a minister's wife."

She gave a short, troubled little laugh, but did not move her eyes.

There was dead silence.

The two people, young in years, but who since early remembrance had balanced each other's needs, in a certain fashion, in the scale of life, stood still, drifting out into the wide ocean of farewell, while they looked earnestly, entirely, for the first time and the last, into each other's eyes. As for Fielding, he saw, though unconsciously, far beyond. He looked into the limpid brown depths of the eyes beseechingly lifted to his, and, as it were, knowing that his heaven lay there, beheld an earthly hell in waiting.

Prudence wished that he would speak — would answer her. Accustomed to his fulfilling, if not anticipating, her slightest wish — accustomed to thinking that Jonas always knew what she was feeling and thinking—she thought his present behavior unaccountable, if not unkind.

"Jonas!" she half whispered. She put out one little hand slowly, and let the tears that gathered under her eyelids fall upon her cheeks.

"My God in heaven!" he said, huskily. He turned away, utterly forgetting that the woman he loved stood there in the flesh, near enough to be touched or scorned by him. The words she had uttered mocked him with the horrid force of a delusion, yet he knew that they were all too powerful and sincere. He crossed the room, and, sitting down before one of the small tables, clinched his fingers mercilessly into some lace beneath them, and buried his face in his hands. For that moment he was supremely, utterly conscious of Self. I think it was the only moment of Jonas Fielding's life in which the needs of his fellow-men made no impression on any fibre of his being. He was absolutely himself, even to the exclusion of Prudence, standing white and tearful in the window. A moment more of silence passed, and then there fluttered vaguely into the young girl's heart a sense that he was in actual pain. The power of his feeling was beyond her, but it was too great not to reach her in some fashion, however feeble.

"Jonas!" she said again; and, still with tears upon her face, she went up, laying one little hand caressingly upon his shoulder. "Do you know what I mean?" she said, in an awe-struck voice. "I think—I know I am unfitted for it. Another woman—even I a little while ago—" She stopped, hardly knowing what to say, for it seemed to her as though explanation must be futile. He raised his face, haggard and worn—old, it seemed to her, in these moments. "Isn't it better to tell you?" she continued, nodding her little head sagely. "Jonas, you would never have wanted to make me wretched—oh! *miserable*—"

"Oh," cried the young man, springing up, "for

Heaven's sake, Prudence, have some mercy! Oh, my child! I free you from our poor, shallow bond. I free you; but let me go with some mercy!"

He stood looking at her, with an air that would have told any other woman something of the maddening feeling in his heart. Prudence looked half frightened, half ashamed.

"You think my head is turned," she said, reproachfully.

"No," said Jonas, "I do not. I see you as you are yourself. All the talking in the world would show me no more than I read in your eyes."

She began to breathe more freely. It was, at all events, some comfort to feel that Jonas was not angry.

"And could I help it, Jo?" she said, forcing her little hand upon his arm. "Oh, I *tried* so hard, and I love you so truly, *truly*—oh, Jonas, you *know* I do!—but I see I'm not made for the life we used to talk about. You will be better without me. You will be glad of my having told you this."

It was, perhaps, an evidence of Fielding's complete understanding of the situation that he continued speechless. How contribute words to so dead a thing as what lay between them and the past? Yet passionately sweet and bitter memories were trying to free themselves from this bondage he was forcing them into, crying out with voices he silenced almost with disdain. Gradually Pru-

dence withdrew from that attitude of soft persua-
siveness. She went over to the fireplace, beginning audibly to cry. Jonas remained standing
where she left him. Then the variation of moods
was nothing to him. He cared as little for his own
physical sensations of actual pain as he cared for
Prudence's weeping. The stronger elements of a
sudden grief were surging within him, and he felt
that he was standing on the very threshold of a
ruinous despair.

"Prudence," he said at last, in a hard voice, and
wrenched himself around facing the girl—"Prudence, tell me one thing on your honor: has there
ever been an hour or a day in which you have
truly loved me?"

Prudence looked at him through a mist of tears.

"Jonas," she said—"Jonas, don't be cross!"

"Cross!" He echoed the word as if it rent his
heart asunder. "Cross, child! I could be nothing ever like that to you. Tell me what I ask; it
may influence all my life."

Prudence paused. She searched furtively the
recesses of her gentle little heart, the background
of gliding years against which this scene rose, her
first genuine moment of perplexity or analysis.
But for one brief, happy summer, a few months
ago—but for this fever of the world's praise to-
day—she might have answered differently. As it
was, "Jonas," she said, contritely, "I don't think I

truly ever did.   But it was only lately, when I saw
this kind of life—"   She glanced around Miss Armory's luxurious room, searching involuntarily for
something which would demonstrate her meaning.
"I like to be comfortable, as they are here.   That
gentleman's rooms—Mr. Simmonson's, I mean—I
enjoy all that, and I *know* I shall miss it."   She
paused again, realizing that all this luxury of form
and color had affected her but partially; but it
served to define her distrust of a grayer life.

Jonas made an appeal suddenly, not to her affec-
tions, but to her possible higher nature.

"And is there nothing else—nothing earnest,
and true, and real, and loving in *my* life?"   He
spoke with passionate bitterness.

"Oh, *Jonas!*" said Prudence, despairingly.

"Prue," he exclaimed—and now he had the
power to go up and look with gentle eyes upon
the girl—"I am going away.   Perhaps I shall not
see you for a long time again.   But remember one
thing: if you need me, I am within call.   I shall
never, never forget one littlest thing.   Dear, it lies
solemnly within me, though you have never seen
it, and I can remember, with the grave above me,
every look of your face, every word and hour we
have had together, every lightest touch of your little hand."   The man's voice trembled; he was too
near the beauty of her richly-tinted face, too near
the tremulous sweetness of her uplifted eyes, not

to feel his heart beating with dangerous swiftness. He stretched his hands out, grasping hers with eager intensity.

"Dear," he said, "I don't know what you mean to do; but I know they want you to marry that man. Pray, pray do not do it." Prue hung her head. "I know he will ask you," Fielding went on, still clinching the girl's wrists; "but if it be so, think, think before you turn away from all you understand in life."

He held her hands, looking at her with a dimmed vision, yet his mind was travelling backward with painful clearness and intensity. He saw all those vanished, futile years with their measure of passion, happiness, and belief, with their meed of daily acts glorified by the sense that they were tending toward the crowning joy of his life. Even in this tumultuous moment something rose in the man's breast like an exultation, in that he had gathered during those very years a spiritual force capable of some resistance against what seemed to him the very damnation of his earthly hopes.

"Prue, Prue, my darling!" he said, hoarsely, "you will not forget it all; some day, dear, I think you will know what this love laid at your feet really was. Don't let it grieve you even then, dear. We —your brother Paul and I—always meant to shield you from care or sorrow; even in this trouble I must fulfil his part. Prue, my child, do not grieve."

Come what would, he felt that he must leave her without that tear-stained face. "I must say good-bye, dear, now. God bless and keep you!"

For an instant—as a bird might remember some summer's resting-place—Prudence felt like putting out a hand for him to take her back; it suddenly flashed upon her what a great part of her life he had been: and he was going forever—leaving her —but this sensation vanished: its traces were a slight pallor, a tremulous sweetness in the eyes, with which she mutely answered his good-bye.

Jonas had no definite intention of any kind when he left Prudence in the brilliant room, and made his way down-stairs. There he tried to collect his thoughts, and in doing so he remembered Helena, recalling her much as one in waking tries to conjure up the faces in a dream. With the recollection of her kindness, her gentle womanliness of yesterday, came a sense that he owed her some explanation of the morning. He had a card in his pocket, and, standing in the hall, he scribbled the following words:

"Please do not speak to Prudence about this morning. We have both made a mistake, that is all. I pray that she may be happy. I will leave London soon, but you shall hear of me before I go to America. I preach for my friend at N—— Sunday fortnight, and after that I shall be a few hours in London. Thank you *always*."

He wrote the words in a stupefied condition, and, asking for an envelope, he enclosed the card to Miss Armory. When he went out into the street, it seemed as if the fresh air of the morning stifled him.

XI.

HE walked on and on for more than two hours, heedless of everything but the impulse of movement, which seemed to make his misery less horrible to bear. Then, in extreme weariness, he found his hotel, and going up into his room, sat down at his table, staring vacantly at the drab-colored wall before him. In the hours of that horrible day he could not define or analyze anything; that his world was changed, absolutely, he knew with an almost mocking clearness; but what was left in it —even what any realities of the past had been— he could not tell. He let the hours pass sitting at the table, not attempting conclusions; not seeking answers to the questions that sometimes made their way across the chaos of his thoughts. So, he fancied, the whole of life might drift by him; purposes, ideals, inspirations seemed gone. He had no more power to desire or hope for anything than he had to change the courses of the heavens or the earth. As the faint wintry dusk gathered, he became conscious, in a dreamy way, that he was cold, and, leaving his chair, he walked about the room, still thinking, thinking, but with no clearer perceptions of what it would all tend to. Passion, with all its highest, most ennobling meanings, had so far held him, joyous or serene, above the pettinesses, the commonplace vexations, of his life. There had been hours of fierce spiritual contest, but never periods of despair, and, moving slowly about the cheerless room, he asked himself whether this was not the moment of supreme test in which he would succumb. Then came moments of sharp, quiet agony, when he thought that henceforth and forever the joy of even remembering Prudence must be denied him; never again could he, sitting at his work, think of the day when if he raised his eyes it might be to encounter hers; never again must he think of her small needs, her tired moments which he might soothe, her joys or her sorrows. To count all these as in some fashion his, had been for years the ardor of his life, and he remembered these parts of his existence with a sense that his dead lay stretched before him; not flower-strewn, except by the blossoms of passionate, agonized memory; not peaceful, save with the calm of despair; not reverently prepared for a tomb at which he might sit, remembering perfect hours which had been his. He could not say—

> "To-morrow, do thy worst, for I have lived to-day;
>   Be fair or foul, or rain or shine,
>   The joys I have possessed, in spite of Fate, are mine."

He had seen the joyousness of life die, and all

that remained was to sit, as it were, watching it
during the gathering hours of the night, until
heaven opened and told him where he should lay
it in a final resting-place. A death resurrectionless
and entire! It seemed to the man as he sat there,
the winter gloom falling thickly about him, as
though the room was peopled with phantoms of
some lurid, delusive past; as if grim shapes hover-
ed around that silent figure which meant his Life;
as if the scenes and hours of the past had taken
on themselves form and motion, mocking him with
voices that rent the air; . . . but a fevered imagi-
nation was new to Fielding, and when the hide-
ousness of such fantasies seized him he would rise
and walk about in the darkness, trying to force
himself into at least a duller frame of mind. What,
he asked himself, what was it he had believed of
her? Never once had he doubted her simple loyalty to their unwritten bond, and in the midst of
his heart-cries Jonas did not rebuke the girl for not
knowing what she did. That he had idealized her,
that she had never really loved him at any moment,
lent only a more mocking shadow to his life. That
he had spent the sweetness of his passion, the fervor of his hopes, the loftiness of his soul, upon an
idea, sharpened the sense of injustice with which
he felt himself oppressed. He had told her that all
the talking in the world would show him no more
than he read in one look of her eyes, and in proof

of this he had never, from the first word, questioned her resolve; not once had it occurred to him
that persuasion would do anything. Five minutes
later, had she come to his arms, he would have re-
jected her. The thing that had seemed his had
died in the first words she uttered.

Time was nothing to him; not even calculable
by heart-throbs in the hours of that weary day
and night. He did not leave his room; he never
thought of food; when the darkness became absolute he lighted his candles, and in doing so his
eyes fell upon a desk in which he had for years
cherished any letters worth remembering. Paul
Marlitt's were among them, and with swift recollection of that fragrant life, so blessed in its ending, and which had meant so much on earth, Jonas
turned, and, opening the desk, took out the faded
packet which he often felt his unseen Mentor.

The letters had been written at odd times. During any separation, Paul had exchanged some word
with his chosen friend, and turning the boldly written pages was like touching the harmonies of tenderly familiar sounds. The clear sweetness of the
past arose; Jonas felt as if he could catch again
the meanings of the notes sounded in his younger
days; he read on, here and there; at first he sought
for mentions of Prudence, but when the name appeared he found it was not possible to read such
sentences. He looked out bits that might have

been Paul's voice, speaking Paul's very self; and then arose a swift vision of Marlitt's clear-eyed gaze, his thin, eager face; the lights and shadows that reflected them told his every pulsation to his friend:

"To-day I walked down by the old canal, keenly enjoying the level sweep of green which stretches on the other side; and it occurred to me how much happiness is to be found in simplicity. When Nature wishes to impress us, she never does it with elaborations: a bit of meadow, a reedy bend in the river, a sky faintly illumined from the west; these would have formed my subjects to-day had I been a painter; and I remembered your advice, and tried to form analogies between this perfection of outward things in nature and the inner workings of the perfectly balanced mind. But while I realized the justice of your theories, I found that Nature had laid hold of me so entirely that she demanded even the yielding up of substrata of thought. I felt curiously serene, and I wish I could send you some of my calmly grateful conclusions. . . . Are you still engrossed by Carlyle? and if so, tell me whether it has reached the final note of the crescendo, which is 'Sartor Resartus' and 'John Sterling.' I think I like nothing better in À Kempis than the forcible illustration in 'Sartor Resartus' of man's insignificance as one of the multitude, and yet his tremendous inner responsibilities—that what is of

importance is only our subjective impress upon
other minds. Sometimes I want to walk to Chelsea in London, if only to touch Carlyle's hand!
After all, Fielding, what *can* we do better than impress other lives, lead others to thought, or action,
or desire, which can ennoble the world? Can you
not imagine being gloriously happy in setting up
conscientious intellect as a sympathetic, eager companion, who shall point out and lead you to paths
others are treading or must tread, and say, do this
or do that, because you will be a help, or a precedent, or a suggestion to those who walk beside you
or come after? Isn't this better than even martyrdom?—or where is there a loud-sounding heroism
like it? . . . I have been arguing your question of
comparison between St. Peter and St. Paul with
K——. He likes St. Peter's large-minded humility; but for myself, I prefer St. Paul's complete ac-
knowledgment of error. It lays hold of me and
fascinates me, and has in it that suggestion of 'up,
up, on, on,' which we lotus-eating minds need. Sedate people, given to few variations of mood or
purpose, perhaps are helped by the more forcible
weakness and swift remorse of St. Peter, but, as you
know, to me work among the multitude is everything, and I feel with St. Paul, acting for all the
world—as well when he cried out slaughter, believing he was right, as in speedily saying, 'Lord, what
wilt thou have me do?' K—— declares that St.

Paul's influence is more intellectual than spiritual;
but to me this only renders the traces and the
words that he has left more beautiful, for to-day is
the day of intellect, and we often need the impulse
first in the brain and heart, giving up soul an easy
conquest later.

"What you say about feeling tired of yourself I
thoroughly appreciate; only what particular difference does it make in a nature which cordially leans
toward the wholesome? Take the mood like any
bad dream or bad feeling. We need all the repose
from self-dissatisfaction of this sort possible, and I
think one can create a clear-cut, cleanly philosophy
for just such depressing occasions. I find it is well
to try and begin something new at such times
which shall be of use to others. Write somebody
a letter; allow some bore to be comfortable at
your expense; or, if you can do it, go into the
country. Nothing ever brings me so quickly to a
sense of humanity and kindness as the sight of
green fields and leafy trees, of some old-fashioned,
radiant garden, which blooms untouched by the
rules and precisions of the landscape garden. Do
you ever get a sense of life being so full with appreciations and desires that these blank hours can
be treated as welcome guests?—the periods of
sweeping out from the brain all the fantastic
things that float in unawares, and clog the chan-
nels of simple, clear-eyed thought?

"I have often wondered what our Creator must think of the way in which some of his creatures use their abilities. To-day I visited M——'s studio, and I felt with old papa Wilson like saying, 'Sir, that sunset is a lie, sir—an abominable falsehood, sir!' but I didn't say it, simply because it occurred to me that my mission was not that of art criticism, and *my* realities might not be *his;* possibly to him those glaring streaks of color represented the same thing that I saw, in faint splendors, in mystical, wonderful harmonies, illumining a western horizon, faintly flooding a palpitating, dusky-tinted world; so I remained silent while he talked, and I thought of you; how strange it is for a man so cleverly analytical as you are *not* to understand that you cannot always find or make people what you would have them. Don't you know that you imagine people *must* be what you think them? I don't think you idealize, but you take for granted. Some of these days some feeling, or belief, or impulse of yours will receive a terrific shock; and then, what then, Fielding — well, the Deluge!

"K—— came in very early to-day, with an important air and a stout stick. I knew immediately it meant a walk in the country, and parsing theology. Now you know how widely he and I differ; yet there is this always to be felt with K——: he is very, very *real;* and he has about him nei-

ther false sentiment, exaggeration, nor pathos of
the weakening sort, which contrives to make one
feel a sense of compassion overcoming clever argu-
ment. This is, I always say to myself, a genuine
man; and in the presence of reality like his, one
properly estimates one's self."

Jonas read on and on, page after page. What
he had thought of at the outset was to put himself
back into the old frame of mind and thought belonging to the days in which Marlitt's words were
written; and undercurrent was the desire to re-
produce some strong sensation, and to force himself to believe that something he had once found a
lofty influence could still remain.

Dead in his grave, with years between him and
visible sympathy, Paul Marlitt accomplished a purpose. Holding the faded papers in his hands,
Jonas woke up to something like belief in a life
to live — to something which, if still shrouded in
gloom, showed the tremulous vibrations of a coming light. The night had passed, and Fielding,
standing up, walked over to the window of his
room and looked out upon the red-streaked wintry
sky — the silent, grayly colored city. Few sounds
were audible; the chill of the daybreak was still
unbroken; but, as he looked, there swept into the
man's soul a feeling that underlying all that silence
was the throbbing of all the world—that stretched

before him were the dumb evidences of a passionate, pulsating humanity, not to be forgotten, not
to be readily cast aside, not to be held worthless
as helps toward perfection, because he needs must
sit beside his dead for the hours of a day and
night, and then lay it reverently forever in God's
keeping.

XII.

MENTION has been made of Miss Armory's widowed cousin, with whom part of every year in our young lady's life was spent. But it was decidedly unusual for this Mrs. Van Leide to arrive and claim Helena for the 1st of February. This year, however, the elder lady had changed her usual plans, and one morning, when Helena had been walking, she returned to find a summons to Boyle's Hotel. Mrs. Van Leide always went to Boyle's. She said it was a family habit, but it was in reality more of a family failing, for at Boyle's ten times as much money was paid for everything as was necessary, and a general sense was diffused among the guests that they were elegant and exclusive at the expense of personal comfort. Mrs. Van Leide, however, was a woman who clung to traditions, and I think she believed in Boyle's as the one permanently English feature in her life.

Helena and her cousin were not only bound by the ties of kinship and frequent companionship, but by those of a purely accidental friendship. They had so much in common, that they frequently regretted the fact that nature and circumstances had forced them into a certain alliance; for choosing each other's companionship would have had for them a flavor of keen discernment and peculiar fitness, which they felt they lost in having a reason in their family connection. When they were separated, they exchanged very analytical letters; and when Helena learned of Mrs. Van Leide's unexpected arrival in London she felt rebuked. Of late she had written so meagrely that the past two months were, so far as genuine life was concerned, a blank.

'Miss Armory went to Boyle's without delay, and her cousin received her warmly. She was a woman scarcely forty, having that look of careful freshness which we are accustomed to think rare among elderly American women, yet which is, I think, a prevailing characteristic in many States. She was blonde, and, if not pretty, had a fascinating smile and extremely fine blue eyes; her manner was perfectly charming, but there was a brisk air about it totally incompatible with her horror of anything unconventional, or out of the accepted fashion of the hour. She declared she got the best of everything which the world could give her, without paying the price of explaining her conduct or ideas. She dressed superbly, and always was eager to counsel Americans abroad as to the best dressmakers and most satisfactory shops; yet her inclinations were chiefly literary. She thoroughly appreciated good work, took in the very subtlest element in American or British humor, and owned to a trifle of "temperament"—just enough to make her feel averse to the society of people who, she said, had "limitations." Helena Armory was avowedly her chosen friend and favorite cousin, so that the girl's orphaned condition was by no means the cause of Mrs. Van Leide's systematic chaperonage.

"Well," Mrs. Van Leide exclaimed, as Miss Armory appeared, "you didn't expect me so soon! To tell you the truth, Helena, I got tired of Berlin, and you hadn't written, and I thought I'd come over. Then I wanted to go to that festival at N——."

Helena gave a start at the words.

"Oh," she said, "I forgot there was to be a festival at N——."

"Of course," answered Mrs. Van Leide; "only it is a little late in the season. Now are you ready to go with me there? My dearest girl, you look horribly pale!"

Helena protested that she was perfectly well, but she certainly looked badly.

"Well," said Mrs. Van Leide, "you see it's well I came over. I knew you wanted looking after."

Helena was standing in the window of the sitting-room which was always devoted to Mrs. Van

Leide's use at Boyle's, and at these words she felt a guilty throb.

"Why, Margaret?" she said, turning toward the elder lady with a smile.

"Well, my reasons are various, but chiefly instinctive. To begin with, you've almost totally neglected writing to me, and I knew if you had not something inexplicable in your mind you would not have been silent."

Helena for a moment occupied herself in studying the pavement of Dover Street. Then she said, slowly,

"Well, I've had a horribly bad conscience. You know I am not usually burdened by my sins, though I acknowledge them freely; but lately something has been crying out within me, and I know I ought to stand here this very minute in sackcloth and ashes."

Mrs. Van Leide regarded her cousin with a fine, appreciative smile. "Go on," she said, admiringly. "What was your sin?"

"I can hardly tell you, because it would involve so many things and people you don't know about."

"I never was obtuse yet, I hope, my dearest."

"No. Well, then, I am afraid I have been the means of ruining the life—of one of the noblest-hearted men I ever knew."

Mrs. Van Leide looked at her for a moment before she said: "You *always* compassionated your

lovers. Why do you regard this particular case as
novel?"

"Oh," cried Helena, averting her face swiftly,
"this man was not my lover!" And then, with
delicacy, she told the outlines of Prue's story, the
events of the last six or eight weeks. To Mrs. Van
Leide the impressive feature was that she knew
Prudence Marlitt's family.

"And I know more of her than you do; for I
was at Lennox last year—when I went home, you
know, for Dolly Barclay's wedding—and there I
heard of another of Prudence Marlitt's love affairs."

Helena stared; her cheeks were pale enough
now, and she was not afraid to come nearer Mrs.
Van Leide.

"Oh yes," pursued that lady; "she had a sort
of love affair with young Maybery. A capital
match he'd be for any girl; and, if I'm not mistaken, he's in London this very moment. Is Prudence actually engaged to this Mr. Simmonson?"

"Oh no; but Mrs. Crane is urging it upon her.
I have only seen her occasionally lately. Just
now she and her aunt are at Holbrook with Lady
Fanny."

Mrs. Van Leide remained a moment thoughtfully considering the position.

"I'm not a particularly patriotic person," she
said, at last, "but I always think transplanting is

doubtful business with most Americans. I believe I'll give George Maybery my address."

Helena had a feeling that prevented her entering into farther responsibilities where the destinies of others were concerned, but she was willing to let Mrs. Van Leide occupy herself as ardently as she chose with George Maybery's affairs. It was no surprise to her, on entering her cousin's sitting-room the following afternoon, to find a tall, good-looking young man standing on the rug, and whom Mrs. Van Leide immediately presented as Mr. Maybery.

Helena had always enjoyed the study of types among the many Americans she met abroad, and this young man was peculiarly interesting. He was the very pleasantest type of a prosperous New Yorker. He bore about with him a flavor of good society and cheerfulness, of a capability for thoroughly enjoying the sunny, busy side of life. He was good-looking, with light hair and a clear gray eye, and his smile and voice and laugh were peculiarly pleasant. He dressed admirably, although his clothes looked new, and Helena did not require to be told that he was a member of a very rich, traditionally great firm. Helena amused herself by fancying that he lived expensively—say on Madison Avenue about Thirty-second Street—that he belonged to the Union Club, and knew better than most Americans what claret a man ought to drink at his dinner. He was thoroughly contented with life, and joyous in his way of receiving its blessings, and before she had talked with him ten minutes Miss Armory perceived that he was violently in love with Prue. He had met her during that one summer in which Prue had been away from Ponkamak, and Helena gathered that some silly interference on the part of Mr. Maybery's sister had broken up what might have been an engagement. His sister came from Ponkamak, and he had known Jonas Fielding at Yale.

"Excellent fellow!" said Mr. Maybery, with his honest, good-humored smile. "I never could cram as he did, but I always enjoyed watching him. He and Paul Marlitt were the David and Jonathan of T——. You never knew him?"

To Helena the man's name had been in a sort of fashion consecrated by the story Jonas had told her. She changed the subject.

"Well, Mr. Maybery," she said, pleasantly, "are you going down to Holbrook to see Prue?"

The young man hesitated a little.

"Well, now," he said, inquiringly, "I suppose I *could* do that over here — just run down there and make a call on a young lady I knew in the house?"

"Oh, certainly; but you may have the way smoother than that. I know Lady Fanny well, and I'll gladly give you a letter to her."

Mr. Maybery expressed himself as much pleased by this; but in some way it was peculiarly distressing to Helena to discuss Prudence Marlitt with any one. She felt jarred by even the slight air of proprietorship in the young man's manner. He was confident, she could see, of success in anything he undertook, and he departed in a most good-humored frame of mind, leaving upon Helena an impression of wholesome, happy prosperity.

"He is just the man to enjoy having his wife admired by every one else," she said to Mrs. Van Leide when they were alone.

"And if Prudence develops into a fine lady of fashion, he'll approve of her all the more."

Margaret Van Leide had been closely studying her cousin since her arrival in London, and her critical faculty seemed to receive a new impetus.

"Helena," she said, meaningly, "are you getting cynical?"

"Getting!" said Helena, with a light laugh. "I think I always was—and tried to be—a little."

"Then you are more so than ever, and I wish you would get married."

"And make the tendency a characteristic?"

"Come, Lena, don't be idiotic."

"I don't mean to be," laughed Helena, "and therefore let us make our conversation more profitable. I came to-day to tell you I am quite ready to start for N—— to-morrow."

Mrs. Van Leide made no answer. She endured ten minutes of silence, looking now and then at her cousin with rebuke or pity in her eyes.

"What did I tell you, Margaret?" said the girl, finally. "That I had a bad conscience. Well, so I have; but I don't think, apart from that, I'm conscious of anything except—that I love you better every day."

As Miss Armory spoke she rose and moved over to the window. When she turned again there were traces of tears upon her face.

XIII.

HELENA ARMORY always declared that with each impression of the English country some new sense of being and exhilaration came to her. Journeying in February to N—— with Mrs. Van Leide was, it seemed to her, the one soothing influence life could just then have offered her. She was not in a mood to demand excitement. The peaceful winter landscape, the solemnities of an English cathedral town, the harmonies of the approaching festival, were all that she demanded of outward things; and that Jonas Fielding was to preach at N—— on Sunday night was remembered at times, with a half-sad conjecture as to how she would find time and the ruin of his hopes had affected him.

The first days at N—— passed by quickly enough. The town is large, but full of sleepy nooks in which red brick and ivy and restless rookeries complete the charm felt here and there and everywhere by the visitor who cares for suggestive architecture and the influence of bricks and mortar. Helena had several hours of each day to herself, when Mrs. Van Leide attended rehearsals, to which she went with her usual zeal. Helena, declaring that she

preferred to take the affair in perfection, devoted
these hours to idle wanderings about the town,
discovering every bit of the old cathedral, and
learning above all things to love the cosy river-
bank, which finds appreciators only, I think, among
artists, who like its gradations of feathery willows
and long stretches of level meadows, its occasional
old warehouses, and queer anchors for the barges
that dreamily come and go. The winter gave no
pallor to this scene, but then the English winter
rarely does that in any place; here, however, the
approach of February had brought about a touch
of spring. There was certainly no warmth, but
growing things looked ready for the hand of loving green to lead them into blossom. There was
almost a fragrance in the cold, still air, and the
sky was radiantly blue, with here and there the
feathery lights of clouds that it seemed never
could mean rain.

Helena did not know then how much she
thought of in those solitary walks in which she
gave herself up to enjoyment of the country; but
later the whole place came back to her, bit by bit,
associated with thoughts that meant the deepest
pulsations of her being. The changing colors on
the bank; the vivid reflections of objects in the
water, growing denser as the daylight waned; the
faint green; the windy meadows; the figures of
boatmen and towns-people passing to and fro; the

crowning solemnity of the cathedral spires, whose
gray tones she caught always on her homeward
walks—all these recurred to her as forces connected with that period of mental conflict—as to be the
eternal associations of moments and hours which
might affect or move forward her whole life. She
had made the acquaintance of the man who rowed
a small ferry-boat across the river at a certain
point, and in two or three days they were on intimate terms of almost friendship. He lived in a
quaint little house with a sixteenth-century window bulging over the river, and his wife, as Helena
soon found out, was bedridden. The man was a
tall, brown-faced countryman, with an imaginative
temperament qualified by the driest, dullest of actual surroundings; but to Helena his very simplicity was refreshing as was the calm stillness of the
country. She told Mrs. Van Leide she was trying to see *real* people, and to find out whether she
were one of them herself, or a terrible imposition.

"If one only could have talked to Adam, for instance!" she remarked.

"But Adam would have been so unsatisfactory,"
answered Mrs. Van Leide—"a man actually inex-
perienced."

"But so deliciously fresh," said Helena. "Sometimes I think I am all warped and distorted from
having lived among so many fascinating suggestions. I am so anxious to discover the real *me*.

Just as I find I am saying or doing something nice or interesting, or foolish or weak-minded, I realize it is because I have seen or heard or felt the suggestion from somebody else."

"And if you discover the real *you*, and find yourself full of a primitive simplicity, what shall you do?"

" I will be charmed," said the girl. " But I'm afraid that will never come to pass. The more I see of my old boatman, the more I realize how far I have drifted away from the clear Puritan stock I came from."

" The most hampered of all people !" ejaculated Mrs. Van Leide, who was herself proudly, intensely Knickerbocker.

Helena made up her mind not to be so analytical that she would allow herself no quiet enjoyment with the old boatman and his wife. She gave herself up to simple, frank talks with them, and asked nothing for effect. Their influence she declared to be wholesome, even if it did not enlighten her ; and the sanded floor of the cottage, the cleanly furniture, the old windows blooming with flowers, the bed with its patient sufferer—all became active influences in her memory when this period was long past. The humble people invested her with no false charm. They had none of that power of idealizing which belongs to the cultured classes. To them she was a " bonny, gentle

young lady," and she *was* all of that. They took
things just as they found them, and gave nothing
a pernicious influence by exaggerating its power
or effect. From her quiet walks and her humble
friendships Helena drifted, with a certain sense of
surprise, into the rushing, splendid harmonies of
the festival. There had been three days of music
that lifted her into the regions of exaltation, when
the Sunday came which she knew would bring
Jonas Fielding to N——.

The day dawned dismally. Toward sunset, as
Helena looked out upon the windy, rain-washed
streets, she wished that he had come when the
peace and calm of the old town might have sooth-
ed him. She wondered if he would not be newly
chilled by confronting a strange town, strange people, when Nature so completely refused her smiles;
but, had she known the truth at that moment, she
would have seen that Fielding's mood was one in
which the elements meant nothing to him. He
had suspended all sense of what affected him outwardly; and as he made his way through the darkening, wet streets of the town, he was thinking only
that he was to be a voice to the people. Lives,
human beings with souls and unborn deeds to be
moved or roused into life by what he might say,
were perhaps waiting. Jonas left cynicism, dainty
philanderings of the mind, fantastic ideas of duty
or well-being, utterly in the background. He had

come from London to N—— by a train that left
him only an hour before the time for service, and
this period he spent in hastily thinking over his
sermon. It was unwritten, yet it had been all
thought out. Had he known that Miss Armory
was to be among his listeners, it would have startled him into some confusion. But why should
the words of his text even be remembered by her
ears?

"*Woe unto thee, Chorazin! woe unto thee, Beth-
saida! for if the mighty works which were done in
you had been done in Tyre and Sidon, they would
have repented long ago in sackcloth and ashes.*"

XIV.

HE had not been ten minutes in the pulpit—
the moderate confusion of an unfamiliar, irregularly
lighted edifice, a large, unknown congregation, was
just passing away—when he became conscious of
eyes, of lips, of the grace of a certain figure he had
seen before, and, peering a little into a space illumined fitfully, he made out that the tranquil, motionless figure and face belonged to Miss Armory.
The man was in that frame of mind which is not
due to mental excitement, yet has the power of
making a surprise almost impossible. He looked
at her without any feeling of wonderment ; he saw,
without thinking of it, the luxurious elegance of
her dress and bearing in the midst of the duller
people about her ; and though he never sought her
eyes, he began and ended his sermon conscious that
she sat there exacting from him his most prophetic. But he had the strong sense of power, the ela-
tion, which a listening multitude give. So far had
the man wrenched himself in the last fortnight
from the need of individuals, that Helena seemed
to him only a stronger, more concentrated, expression of human needs ; the faces of the crowd never

closed hers in, yet it seemed to him only as though by some subtle power she was the final emphasis of their wants. Gradually the girl's shining eyes and sweet, high-bred face grew to him luminously significant. She seemed, with her earnest look, to be saying, " I am part of a need—a need belonging to all this palpitating multitude of poor humanity."

Jonas, as I have said, preached from only a few hurried notes, so that he kept no record of that sermon. Later, he could not have put any of its sentences together, but it seemed always to express some new era in his life. There was an absolute freedom from the sensational, yet the tension of the past fortnight had resulted in a peculiar elevation of thought, and he poured forth his words with a direct appeal to the rarely stirred and more exalted regions of the human soul. His voice startled Helena by its sweetness. There was a cadence in it that would have given harsher words a charm; but, tremendous as was his text, he had little that was denunciatory in his discourse. That " Woe to Chorazin" he applied to every human soul, forming one of a multitude, and he called upon his hearers to bear without despondency, to be exalted without mock enthusiasm, to be active without exaggerations. These were simple suggestions, yet he endowed them with the richness of his own recent mental and spiritual experiences; out of the chaos of his misery and bewilderment he had come with

certain new simple forces, which he gave freely,
nay, joyously, to others. He said he meant to
preach simplicity; and the disjointed sensations of
the past few weeks seemed to have resulted in
calm, clearly-flowing lines. As he preached, he
dimly remembered scenes through which he had
passed — scenes which a merely casual observer
might have been only amused by, but which to
Jonas Fielding, of Ponkamak, in one way typified
that "Chorazin" of old of which the prophetic Woe
had been uttered. He did not mean to impress
any of his hearers with horror or dismay; he preached, as I say, intensely conscious of one hearer; of
the soft, eager face, full of indefinable charm, and
which was perhaps the nearest approach to a purely æsthetic influence he had ever felt; yet his words
were uttered for all those about her, and at his
heart was a passionate demand for absolute sincerity and single-mindedness. The effect of everything he had seen and felt of late was to make him
long to clear from his mind and heart and soul all
that was not grandly simple. He had a sensation
that the best and truest things were the most easily understood, yet that they lay shrouded, hidden,
distorted by the fancies and follies of the to-day in
human weakness. Had he in his mind any hours
which he had passed through when he gently but
eagerly told his listeners of that simple means to
perfection? As I have said, vague memories of

the last few weeks floated into his mind, oppress-
ing him for moments, but he was unconscious that
he meant more than an elaboration of the text
which should impress others as it had always impressed him.   He believed, in fact, that he was
using no arguments which had specially applied to
himself, strongly conscious that he must shake off
forever the influence of prejudice.   Personally the
man's strong face and figure were deeply impressive.   Helena had seen at once that he was haggard and worn, that he had strangely depressed
lines about his mouth and eyes; but this she had
expected; she had almost dreaded to see him;
but what burst upon her as entirely unlooked for
was the magnetism, the power, in his manner.   His
voice rung through the building, and yet it had a
cadence that was like a whisper.   He was utterly
self-forgetful.   To Helena he seemed to be the
concentration of many forces which she had been,
as it were, half conscious of within herself.

The rain was beating violently against the tall
windows of the chapel as Jonas finished his sermon.   Service being ended, Helena moved quietly
away, followed by her maid.   She had written a
few lines on a card, and sent them into the vestry-
room for Jonas, and she now half regretted that
she had not asked him to come to their hotel that
evening, for she felt the impulse to see and talk to
him stronger as the time went on.   The tranquil-

"GOD BLESS YOU!"

lity which had possessed her of late seemed to have vanished. She was throbbing with excitement; she defined nothing, made no distinctions between the joyous and the remorseful, the exalted and the depressed. She was simply full of strange emotions, and was bewildered by both them and herself. The carriage from the hotel was waiting, and she was standing in the porch of the chapel securing her wraps a little more conveniently, and as well peering into the wet darkness, to be sure the door of the vehicle was comfortably held open, when she heard her name spoken, and looked up to meet Fielding's gaze near her own. It was so sudden an answer to thought, that she smiled almost tearfully. The young man looked down at her with a kindly, gentle gaze.

"I am so much obliged to you for letting me know that you were here," he said, in a voice which yet held the vibrations of half an hour ago; "and I will surely come to-morrow at ten o'clock, as you said. I thank you." He had taken her hand a moment in his, and as he let it fall he said, in a tone Helena always remembered, "God bless you!"

She made no effort to speak, but she looked at him earnestly.

Every line of his tall figure and strong face in the rain and wind she remembered long after that night had passed away. Indeed, trifles connected with the scene recurred later to her mind with passionate distinctness: the shining, wet pavements; the crowd of curious, eager people coming out of the chapel, some of whom turned for a glance at the elegant young lady to whom the American minister was speaking; the vista beyond the chapel door, irregularly lighted, part growing sombre from desertion; Jonas's final glance in her carriage window; and then some queer thought of her own hands lying on her lap clasped with unconsciously painful intensity.

XV.

FOR days afterward Mrs. Van Leide deplored
the fact that one of "her" headaches prevented
her from seeing Jonas Fielding when he called at
the "George." Helena's account of him had been
very meagre, yet her cousin had felt an ardent
desire to see him for herself. It must have been
that, in spite of chilling words, Helena's testimony
had been to the man's credit; for once Mrs. Van
Leide had exclaimed, "He must be fascinating."

"Fascinating!" Helena had echoed. "Is he?
He is, I think, only intensely real."

Jonas Fielding knew very vaguely that Miss Armory was stopping with a cousin, and he made his
way to the old-fashioned inn, thinking entirely of
the younger lady. The court-yard of the "George"
is very picturesque: there is a paved centre, a wall
richly hung with ivy, an old well, and a sun-dial,
from which both shadows and gleams of light seem
to emanate. Servants were running here and there
on eager duty, but Miss Armory's name produced
instant attention. The American ladies were es-
tablished in the best rooms in the house. They
had a maid and a man servant, and were liberal in

their ideas about shillings and half-crowns. Jonas
had never been more respectfully treated than
when he was led through the corridors of the
"George" to a door-way through which Helena's
voice sounded in a faint "Come in." The room
overlooked the High Street of the town by means
of three old-fashioned windows, with lattice-framed
panes of glass and heavy oaken seats. In one of
them Miss Armory was seated, and, as she turned
her face toward Jonas, she said, simply, "I was
watching for you; you must have come another
way."

"I paid a visit or two with the minister's wife,"
he answered, "and I came in by the lower entrance."

Just as in that first visit to her boudoir in London, Jonas took up his place against the chimney-
piece. Perhaps it was the familiar action, possibly
the sight of his worn face, that made Helena's
heart beat for a moment so that it was hard to
speak. She moved about the room a little. It was
cumbrously but well furnished with the oak and
carvings of two hundred years ago, the ornaments
in needle-work and painting to which time only
has given a certain authority for existence. She
looked as if she wanted to gather either inspiration or courage, and it seemed as if she found it
in Fielding's simple, unaverted gaze. She stopped
in the window nearest him, and said, passionately,

"Do you hate me? Tell me—oh, if in justice to truth you can — tell me if I have injured your life!"

Fielding looked with an eager light at her. "No, no, no!" he said, quickly. "Oh, has this been troubling you? Oh no, indeed! I understand it all; I have thought it all out. I know now that I ought better to have understood many things. There is no one to blame. I am simply paying for arrogance, for blindness, and perhaps it has helped me to a better life."

Helena sat still, regarding him with a fixed, gentle vision.

"Do not imagine," he continued, "that I have not spent hours and days in bitter rebellion"— the remembrance brought back a look of torture to his face—"only now I know that in resigning or conforming myself to these circumstances I shall do all that is left to me to do. I shall be fulfilling some need within me, answering, perhaps, to some need in others."

Helena's lips opened to say, "And you are happy?" but she hesitated, and substituted, "You feel it is God's will?"

Jonas looked into space, with a quiet, thoughtful smile.

"No," he said, "I can scarcely say that, because it seems to me that in certain ways our deeds are our own. He tells us that we must be vigilant

11

and earnest and single-minded. If by my own blindness I have misinterpreted things, have built up a temple of clay in my heart—well, I must not take that mock-consolation to myself, and go about feeling my inner martyrdom the result only of *His* will. I must say I conform myself to the facts of my life because He has *permitted* them. I do not believe He designs these miseries which come from our own stupidity, idleness, or wickedness."

Helena listened intently. When he had finished she turned her gaze from the sunny street, smiling faintly.

"You are—cruelly strong," she said.

Fielding started slightly forward. "Oh, do not say or think that!" he exclaimed. "I have only gathered together every force, trying not to be pitifully weak. If I still see life and work ahead of me, do you not think I shall sometimes be chased by the phantoms of the past?—those insecure, restless demons that are so ready to seize upon our depressed or obscured moments, especially if we are forced to live lives for other people. I must never cease the patient toiling after strength. If I were forced to live among exaggerations, it would be my ruin. My hope lies in an existence of simple meanings, pure beliefs."

He spoke with quick insistence, as if commanding acceptance of his words.

"And I," said Helena, slowly—"I am, I suppose,

living among exaggerations? What shall I do?
Do you think I ought to leave it all?"

"No. You and I have different needs; but you
ought to understand things better; you ought to
learn to know gold from dross. You accept too
much; you"—he stopped short, and came over to
the window—"you let the pagan part of life triumph, as it were, over your better self too often.
There is good in that æstheticism, as you call it,
but you ought not to seek relief from the weight
or burdens of nobler impulses in its exaggerations.
How much of it is *real*, ascertain that — *real*, in
either feeling, or action, or good influence. Ascertain that, and then drape it in the richest, softest colors you can find."

He returned to the fireplace, and met her gaze
again with simple kindliness. Helena felt impelled
to say much more to him. She had the confusing
sense that he stood there for one of the permitted
moments in our lives when human beings can reach
each other's very souls for good. She wanted to extract, as it were, some domineering principle of his
philosophy. Might he not, at least, leave her with
some surer impetus toward light? She felt tortured
by the sense that she was losing her opportunity.

"And you do not think a life like mine, for instance, need be worthless — I mean according to
such standards as yours?" She spoke with a note
like a sob in her voice.

"Oh," answered Fielding, almost sadly, "your life ought to be perfect—exquisite." He smiled upon her. "It has done me good, and I shall like to think of it — always. If I have seemed to think of other things for you, it has been because I know so well the richness of possibility in you, the impulses for good you were casting aside."

Helena moved about for a moment before she spoke again; then she said, gravely, "I am haunted now by just that very thing: I *feel* that I have turned aside."

He said nothing.

"It is such a dreadful thing," she went on, "to be pursued by a sense that you have forsaken your earliest ambitions—that your old ideals are mocking you. Sometimes I try to believe they were nothing — the fantastic follies of an unformed mind; but I know better." She stopped, and added, simply, "I think it is you who have made me know better."

"But," he persisted, in a very quiet voice, "do not confuse remorse or regret with too much self-analysis; the rules of a Higher Life for any one of us are grandly simple. You see you have been trying to live on theories, emotions, harmonies. All these can be beautiful and helpful enough, if we grant a substratum of calm, well-measured, simple beliefs. Then the tendency toward paganism

in this intense idea of civilization cannot over-
come us."

"And is this philosophy?" she said, gravely.

"If you ask me," he answered, "I will say that
it is mine; and I think you might be happier in
making it yours. We *must* make the best of our-
selves; we are part of a grand scheme of creation,
of life. Therefore seek a way, and follow it with
all the simplicity and truth you can harbor—"

Helena's eyes were fixed upon him sadly.

"Do you think one is apt to overestimate the
flowers, the fragrances, of an intellectual life?" she
asked, half timidly.

"How can that be?" he exclaimed. "But the
evil of this æsthetic movement is that it tortures
every sentiment either with analysis or sensuous-
ness. The honest fibre of the thing is lost. To
my way of thinking, one of the weak outcomes
of this tendency to-day is a mind like your friend
Simmonson's."

She remained silent for a moment, while Fielding continued to stand looking down upon her
figure and half-averted face. He noticed, as she
stood against the light, that the curve of her cheek
had grown very thin—its usual brilliancy was quite
gone.

"You have not been well," he said, earnestly.
"What is it? Have you been letting all these
things prey upon you?"

"I think perhaps I have," Helena answered. "But I am not at all really ill. Do you remember what you once wrote to me"—and her smile reached her eyes wistfully—"that we must have our periods of mental and moral shock once in so often?"

The past seemed to be across such a gulf of misery that even this slight allusion to one of its expressive moments hurt him.

She went on: "Well, I am having one of mine now, I think; and I believe it will do me good. I shall remember all that you have said—all you have been."

He looked at her with quick comprehension and gratitude. After a few moments' silence, he said, very quietly, "Have you seen—her—since?"

"Twice," answered Helena. "But I remembered what you asked of me—only I tried to be judicious and earnest in my advice."

"Thank you." Fielding spoke with an almost painful distinctness. "I had a note from her this morning." He touched the breast pocket of his coat, hesitated for a barely perceptible moment, and then handed it to Helena.

She read it slowly, standing away from him. It was a childish, gentle, pretty little letter, and told of her engagement to George Maybery. Helena folded it up without comment, and Jonas replaced it.

"She will be very happy," he said at last. "She met him a year ago at Lennox. I believe they had something like an understanding then—at least, I have heard so. Mrs. Crane has explained it to me. I want to make something perfectly clear to your mind, Miss Armory. The more I think of it, the more I see that it has all happened providentially, that she was so admired and sought after here. Marlitt was perfectly right. I think," Fielding added, with a sad smile—"I think he must have *seen* how it would be; at all events, he had keen perceptions—and he loved us both."

Helena made no answer to this. She had resumed her seat in the window, and looking at him sadly, she asked, "And you—what are you going to do?"

"What my hand finds to do, I hope," he said, with an effort at cheerfulness. "And may I ask you the same question?"

"I am going just now to the Pyrenees with my cousin," she answered. "But that is only half an answer to your question. My life has not its decisive duties like yours. I think I shall wait a little while and see."

He looked at her very earnestly. "I should like sometimes to hear from you," he said, a little formally, "and perhaps some day you will be in America. You said, if you remember, that we made a great many beginnings and no endings.

Yet I think that it is not quite true of to-day; perhaps we shall do each other future good. At all events, I say, God bless you! when I thank you for all that you have done."

He held his hand out for good-bye. Helena felt a mist of tears in her eyes, but she was perfectly herself when she answered: "Good-bye—no, *auf wiedersehen!*" She smiled steadily, and spoke with a grave, sweet composure. "Do not make me feel too remorseful by thanking me. Let me thank you, my friend. Yes, you shall hear of me whenever you write."

She gave him her hand, and he held it for a moment very reverently.

It seemed to Helena that when the mist faded from her eyes he was gone.

XVI.

PRUDENCE MARLITT had a quiet little wedding just before Helena and Mrs. Van Leide started for the Pyrenees. The two ladies came back from N—— in order to be of use to the young girl and her aunt in those exciting and important preparations which for so many women create the fascination of such an event. It was odd to see how completely Prudence forsook her brief period of æsthetic light. "George," it appeared, had during these few weeks of his engagement expressed a great many views. He had definite ideas upon female apparel, and Prue rigidly followed them, so that, as Mrs. Maybery, it might be inferred, Prudence would observe critically the very newest fashion. It jarred upon Helena that the young girl made fun of the dainty gowns she had worn at Mrs. Boyce's *conversazione* that night, which now seemed a lifetime ago to Miss Armory; but then in those weeks a great many things jarred upon her. She declared to Mrs. Van Leide that she believed that in five years no one would live in the same house with her, but in truth Margaret Van Leide

had never found her half so lovely or so self-forgetful.

As a companion the older woman had always
considered Helena perfect, but she confessed to
herself that a new charm of some indefinable sort
was added. It was soft and womanly, and seemed
to have its expression in the tender look of her
eyes, the readiness to do little services for Prudence or for any one about her, the very way in
which she moved and spoke and laughed. It was
at that time that Mrs. Van Leide discovered Helena's possible self, and began to lament that years
before she had laughed at her large philanthropical schemes. Something had revealed to her
what real action might have been to this woman,
and Mrs. Van Leide found herself at moments
shrinking from Helena's mutely questioning gaze.
For how much inaction was she accountable, since
she knew she had contributed at all times to the
lotus-eating element which she had found so delightful in Helena's richly colored life and nature?

There could not be said to have been any perceptible jar between the two. I think they felt
drawn even more closely to each other by this
sense that in the past some things might have
been more wisely or less arrogantly ordered ; and
each was too conscious of the other's delicacy of
feeling to formulate what must, if spoken, contain
a rebuke. So the time went on, possessing a heal-

"IT WAS ODD TO SEE HOW COMPLETELY PRUDENCE FORSOOK HER
BRIEF PERIOD OF ÆSTHETIC LIGHT."

ing influence where people are in soul generously sympathetic; and Mrs. Van Leide knew, in spite of her misgivings, that she was dearer to her friend and cousin than she had ever been before, although the younger woman would never again consider her decisions or opinions as infallible. We measure a great many things accurately when we discover our own weaknesses for the first time.

The days rushed by to every one concerned in preparing for the wedding, and led at last to the date when Mr. Maybery conducted his bride out of St. George's and back to Cornwall Gardens, where Mrs. Boyce had insisted the wedding breakfast should be. Everything went off as smoothly and comfortably as possible. Mrs. Crane was a trifle less eager than usual, being overawed, it has always been supposed, by a certain magnificence in Margaret Van Leide's manner, and the fact that Mr. Maybery was a man who took all his wishes and demands so cheerfully for granted. That Barley Simmonson had gone to Algiers was a source of content to the bride. Indeed, everything seemed to please her. Not a shadow once rested on her exquisite face, and it may be inferred that none ever will.

It was three months later that, in the Pyrenees, at Saint-Jean-de-Luz, one day Miss Armory suddenly encountered Barley Simmonson and his friend

Field Mowbray, Jun. The two young men were sketching in the old church, but turned delighted faces upon Miss Armory and her cousin. The solemn architecture and dusky colors about them had evidently palled upon our friend Barley, who had been making very poor attempts at architectural drawing, and became easily social in his manner before they had left the church door. It rather surprised Helena that, after exchanging a few commonplaces, Mr. Simmonson spoke of Prudence, for three months might obliterate the memories of a lifetime with this young man. He walked with Helena into the square, following Mrs. Van Leide and young Mowbray, growing more like himself as they stood in the sunshine and bloom of that sad old city. He seemed interested in hearing certain details of little Prue's engagement and wedding. Helena gave them coldly, in chroniclers' fashion, thinking, indeed, of other things as she stood looking at the sea stretched before them — certainly a finer, handsomer creature, Barley was thinking, than he remembered her in London ; but later the conversation was more vivid and more interesting.

Mrs. Van Leide and Helena were, for the time, occupying the villa of a friend at Biarritz, and in the course of the same evening the young men reappeared. The night was brilliantly fine, and they all strolled into the garden overlooking the stretch of tempestuous, moonlit water. Mr. Simmonson again reverted to Prudence. Sitting upon one of the marble terraces, he told all the party the story of his disappointed love. He detailed it as though he related the pathetic history of some heart-broken friend. The rich fragrances of the garden, possibly the grace of Miss Armory's figure as it was outlined in the warm, soft air, seemed to inspire him; and, sitting above a bank of roses, his graceful beauty was, if possible, more Greek than ever. Helena remarked that he only needed a mandolin to make it perfect. It all sounded very pretty and like a poem. Mrs. Van Leide was quite fascinated.

"And was this girl really such a marvel?" she inquired.

"I will tell you what she was," said Helena, turning round quickly. "We intended her to be a great success; and she was one, after a fashion, only she never once saw the real meaning of anything in English society. Gradually, I believe, the æsthetes found this out. If we taught her a rôle, she was happy to play it; but it was always a rôle. Just as Mr. Benison said, she was only 'a little darling.'"

Barley Simmonson listened, with his eyes upon the sea. He had been moved by his own recital. He thoroughly enjoyed its effect upon himself. There was silence, except for the movement of

the waves upon the beach, until he said, dreamily,
"She was so rare—so rare!"

Helena had carried a letter from Jonas Fielding
all the evening, unopened, in her pocket. When
they had bidden the young men good-night, and
were lingering in the drawing-room, whose windows opened to the fragrances of spring flowers,
Mrs. Van Leide said, suddenly, "What did your
friend Mr. Fielding write?"

"I don't know yet," said Helena, smiling. "Barley Simmonson put me out of tune."

Helena almost involuntarily touched the letter
with her fingers, while Mrs. Van Leide said, "That
young man is uncommonly handsome. Isn't he
Lord Bairham's heir?" Then, seeing that Miss
Armory continued silently preoccupied, she added: "Do you know, Helena, I am afraid you mean
to drift away from the golden chances of youth?
Now, listen to me. You are young and handsome,
and well enough off, and I'd rather have you with
me day and night than any being on earth; yet I
feel as if I, perhaps, had done more to talk you out
of—well, any career—and you ought to have married. You ought to marry now. You—are you
listening, dearest?"

Mrs. Van Leide was sitting by the piano at the
lower end of the pretty room, with its shining floor
and luxury of flowers and color. While she had
been talking Helena had remained motionless in

the open window, her fingers idly touching the roses that hung in languid clusters at her side; but now she turned and crossed the room, slowly kneeling down at her cousin's side, and in her face, lifted earnestly to the older woman's, was something stronger than anything she could have said.

"Margaret, dear," the girl said, very gently, "you will not think me hard, or that I am repressing confidences with you of all people on earth; but you must not grieve in that way over me any more— never ask me to marry any one again. Perhaps some day, when we are old women, in caps and spectacles, and I've a reputation for something very useful"—they smiled wistfully at each other —"I'll tell you my reasons why, but not now, not just now: only never think of it again."

"My child, is it to be like this?"

Helena, holding her friend's hands closely, nodded and smiled, with tears lying under her dark lashes.

"I think—yes, I *think* it must be." But of this, though she says nothing, Mrs. Van Leide is not entirely sure.

THE END.

SOME POPULAR NOVELS

Published by HARPER & BROTHERS, New York.

The Novels in this list which are not otherwise designated are in Octavo, pamphlet form, and may be obtained in ha'f-binding [leather backs and pasteboard sides], suitable for Public and Circulating Libraries, at 25 cents, net, per volume, in addition to the price of the respective works as stated below. The Duodecimo Novels are bound in Cloth, unless otherwise specified.

For a FULL LIST OF NOVELS *published by* HARPER & BROTHERS. *see* HARPER'S NEW AND REVISED CATALOGUE, *which will be sent by mail, postage prepaid, to any address in the United States, on receipt of nine cents*

PRICE

BENEDICT'S John Worthington's Name..................................$ 75
                                              Cloth 1 25
    Miss Dorothy's Charge.. 75
                                              Cloth 1 25
    Miss Van Kortland... 60
                                              Cloth 1 10
    Mr. Vaughan's Heir... 75
    My Daughter Elinor... 80
                                              Cloth 1 30
    St. Simon's Niece... 60
                                              Cloth 1 10
BULWER'S Alice... 35
    A Strange Story. Illustrated................................. 50
                                             12mo 1 25
    Devereux.. 40
    Ernest Maltravers... 35
    Eugene Aram... 35
    Godolphin... 35
                                             12mo 1 50
    Harold, the Last of the Saxon Kings......................... 60
    Kenelm Chillingly... 50
                                               12mo 1 25
    Leila... 25
                                               12mo 1 00
    Lucretia.. 40
    My Novel.. 75
                               2 vols. 12mo 2 50
    Night and Morning.. 50
    Paul Clifford... 40
    Pausanias the Spartan.. 25
                                               12mo 75
    Pelham.. 40
    Rienzi.. 40
    The Caxtons... 50
                                               12mo 1 25
    The Coming Race........................12mo, Paper 50
                                              Cloth 1 00
    The Disowned... 50
    The Last Days of Pompeii....................................... 25
                                             4to, Paper 15
    The Last of the Barons... 50
    The Parisians. Illustrated..................................... 60
                                              12mo 1 50
    The Pilgrims of the Rhine...................................... 20
    What will He do with it ?....................................... 75
                                              Cloth 1 25
    Zanoni.. 35

PRICE

BULWER'S (Robert—"Owen Meredith") The Ring of Amasis
                                                     12mo$1 50
BRADDON'S (Miss) An Open Verdict........................... 35
    A Strange World.. 40
    Asphodel.............................4to, Paper 15
    Aurora Floyd.. 40
    Barbara; or, Splendid Misery................4to, Paper 15
    Birds of Prey. Illustrated................................. 50
    Bound to John Company. Illustrated................ 50
    Charlotte's Inheritance.................................. 35
    Dead Men's Shoes.. 40
    Dead Sea Fruit. Illustrated............................. 50
    Eleanor's Victory.. 60
    Fenton's Quest. Illustrated............................. 50
    Hostages to Fortune. Illustrated...................... 50
    John Marchmont's Legacy............................. 50
    Joshua Haggard's Daughter. Illustrated.............. 50
    Just as I Am...............................4to, Paper 15
    Lost for Love. Illustrated.............................. 50
    Mistletoe Bough, 1878. Edited by M. E. Braddon. 4to, Paper 15
    Mistletoe Bough, 1879. Edited by M. E. Braddon. 4to, Paper 10
    Publicans and Sinners................................... 50
    Strangers and Pilgrims. Illustrated.................... 50
    Taken at the Flood....................................... 50
    The Cloven Foot...........................4to, Paper 15
    The Lovels of Arden. Illustrated........................ 50
    To the Bitter End. Illustrated.......................... 50
    Vixen......................................4to, Paper 15
    Weavers and Weft.. 25
BRONTÉ'S (Charlotte) Jane Eyre........................... 40
                                     Illustrated. 12mo 1 00
                                      4to, Paper 15
    Shirley... 50
                                     Illustrated. 12mo 1 00
    The Professor. Illustrated.......................12mo 1 00
    Villette.. 50
                                     Illustrated. 12mo 1 00
    (Anna) The Tenant of Wildfell Hall. Illustrated.......12mo 1 00
    (Emily) Wuthering Heights. Illustrated.............12mo 1 00
CRAIK'S (Miss G. M.) Dorcas...................4to, Paper 15
    Mildred.. 30
    Anne Warwick.. 25
    Hard to Bear... 30
    Sydney....................................4to, Paper 15
    Sylvia's Choice... 30
    Two Women................................4to, Paper 15
COLLINS'S (Mortimer) The Vivian Romance...................... 85

PRICE

COLLINS'S Antonina...$ 40
  Armadale. Illustrated.. 60
  Man and Wife. Illustrated.. 60
                            4to, Paper 15
  My Lady's Money......................................32mo, Paper 25
  No Name. Illustrated.. 60
  Percy and the Prophet..............................32mo, Paper 20
  Poor Miss Finch. Illustrated.................................. 60
  The Law and the Lady. Illustrated........................... 50
  The Moonstone. Illustrated.................................... 60
  The New Magdalen... 30
  The Two Destinies. Illustrated............................... 35
  The Woman in White. Illustrated............................. 60
COLLINS'S Illustrated Library Edition...............12mo, per vol. 1 25
  After Dark, and Other Stories. — Antonina. — Armadale. — Basil. — Hide-and-Seek. — Man and Wife. — My Miscellanies. — No Name. — Poor Miss Finch. — The Dead Secret. — The Law and the Lady. — The Moonstone. — The New Magdalen. — The Queen of Hearts. — The Two Destinies. — The Woman in White.

DICKENS'S NOVELS. Illustrated.

A Tale of Two Cities....	50	Nicholas Nickleby..........	1 00
	Cloth 1 00		Cloth 1 50
Barnaby Rudge.........	1 00	Oliver Twist................	50
	Cloth 1 50		Cloth 1 00
Bleak House...........	1 00	Our Mutual Friend........	1 00
	Cloth 1 50		Cloth 1 50
Christmas Stories......	1 00	Pickwick Papers...........	1 00
	Cloth 1 50		Cloth 1 50
David Copperfield......	1 00	4to, Paper	20
	Cloth 1 50	Pictures from Italy, Sketches by Boz, and American	
Dombey and Son.......	1 00	Notes....................	1 00
	Cloth 1 50		Cloth 1 50
Great Expectations.....	1 00	The Old Curiosity Shop......	75
	Cloth 1 50		Cloth 1 25
Little Dorrit..........	1 00	The Uncommercial Traveller,	
	Cloth 1 50	Hard Times, and Edwin	
Martin Chuzzlewit......	1 00	Drood....................	1 00
	Cloth 1 50		Cloth 1 50

Harper's Household Dickens, 16 vols., Cloth, in box, $22 00. The same in 8 vols., Cloth, $20 00; Imitation Half Morocco, $22 00; Half Calf, $40 00.

HUGO'S Ninety-Three. Illustrated................................ 25
                    12mo 1 75
  The Toilers of the Sea....................................... 50
              Illustrated. Cloth 1 50

8 *Harper & Brothers' Popular Novels.*

PRICE

MY Heart's in the Highlands......................4to, Paper $ 10
NICHOLS'S The Sanctuary. Illustrated....................12mo 1 50
NOEL'S (Lady) Owen Gwynne's Great Work.................. 30
    From Generation to Generation.....................4to, Paper 15
NORRIS'S Heaps of Money..................................... 25
NORTON'S (Mrs.) Stuart of Dunleath......................... 35
NOTLEY'S (F. E. M.) Love's Crosses.................4to, Paper 15
    Time Shall Try......................................4to, Paper 15
OLIPHANT'S (Mrs.) Agnes.................................... 50
    A Son of the Soil...................................... 50
    Athelings.. 50
    Brownlows 50
    Caritá... 50
    Chronicles of Carlingford............................. 60
    Days of My Life...............................12mo 1 50
    For Love and Life..................................... 50
    Harry Joscelyn..................................4to, Paper 20
    He That Will Not when He May.............4to, Paper 15
    Innocent. Illustrated................................. 50
    John: a Love Story.................................... 25
    Katie Stewart... 20
    Lucy Crofton..................................12mo 1 50
    Madonna Mary... 50
    Miss Marjoribanks..................................... 50
    Mrs. Arthur... 40
    Ombra 50
    Phœbe, Junior 35
    Squire Arden.. 50
    The Curate in Charge.................................. 20
    The Fugitives..................................4to, Paper 10
    The Greatest Heiress in England...............4to, Paper 15
    The House on the Moor.........................12mo 1 50
    The Laird of Norlaw...........................12mo 1 50
    The Last of the Mortimers.....................12mo 1 50
    The Minister's Wife................................... 50
    The Perpetual Curate................................. 50
        Cloth 1 00
    The Primrose Path..................................... 50
    The Quiet Heart....................................... 20
    The Story of Valentine and his Brother.................. 50
    Within the Precincts...........................4to, Paper 15
    Young Musgrave. 40
ORRED'S (Meta) A Long Time Ago............................ 25
    Honor's Worth.................................4to, Paper 15
PATRICK'S (Mary) Christine Brownlee's Ordeal ....4to, Paper 15
    Marjorie Bruce's Lovers............................... 25
    Mr. Leslie of Underwood.......................4to, Paper 15

PRICE

PAYN'S (Jas.) A Beggar on Horseback......................$ 35

    A Confidential Agent.................... ....4to, Paper 15

    A Grape from a Thorn...........................4to, Paper 20

    A Woman's Vengeance................................. 35

    At Her Mercy...................................... 30

    Bred in the Bone.................................. 40

    By Proxy.. 35

    Carlyon's Year.................................... 25

    Cecil's Tryst..................................... 30

    Found Dead.. 25

    From Exile..4to, Paper 15

    Gwendoline's Harvest.............................. 25

    Halves.. 30

    High Spirits......................................4to, Paper 15

    Less Black than We're Painted..................... 35

    Murphy's Master................................... 20

    One of the Family................................. 25

    The Best of Husbands.............................. 25

    Under One Roof....................................4to, Paper 15

    Walter's Word..................................... 50

    What He Cost Her.................................. 40

    Won—Not Wooed..................................... 35

READE'S Novels: Household Edition. Ill'd........12mo. per vol. 1 00

A Simpleton and The Wandering Heir.	It is Never Too Late to Mend.
A Terrible Temptation.	Love me Little, Love me Long.
A Woman-Hater.	Peg Woffington, Christie Johnstone, &c.
Foul Play.	Put Yourself in His Place.
Griffith Gaunt.	The Cloister and the Hearth.
Hard Cash.	White Lies.

READE'S (Charles) A Hero and a Martyr................... 15

    A Simpleton... ... 35

    A Terrible Temptation. Illustrated................ 40

    A Woman-Hater. Illustrated........................ 60

                            12mo 1 00

    Foul Play... 35

    Griffith Gaunt. Illustrated....................... 40

    Hard Cash. Illustrated............................ 50

    It is Never Too Late to Mend...................... 50

    Love Me Little, Love Me Long...................... 35

    Peg Woffington, &c................................ 50

    Put Yourself in His Place. Illustrated............ 50

    The Cloister and the Hearth....................... 50

    The Jilt..32mo, Paper 20

    The Wandering Heir. Illustrated 25

    White Lies.. 40

SCOTT'S (Sir Walter) Novels. See *Waverley Novels.*

PRICE

RICE & BESANT'S By Celia's Arbor. Illustrated.....8vo, Paper $ 50
Shepherds All and Maidens Fair.....................32mo, Paper   25
Sweet Nelly, My Heart's Delight....................4to, Paper   10
The Chaplain of the Fleet.........................4to, Paper   20
The Golden Butterfly...   40
'Twas in Trafalgar's Bay..........................32mo, Paper   20
When the Ship Comes Home.........................32mo, Paper   25
ROBINSON'S (F. W.) A Bridge of Glass........................   30
A Girl's Romance, and Other Stories......................   30
As Long as She Lived.....................................   50
Carry's Confession.......................................   50
Christie's Faith.............................12mo 1 75
Coward Conscience........................4to, Paper   15
For Her Sake. Illustrated.................................   60
Her Face was Her Fortune.................................   40
Little Kate Kirby. Illustrated...........................   50
Mattie: a Stray..   40
No Man's Friend..   50
Othello the Second.......................32mo, Paper   20
Poor Humanity..   50
Poor Zeph !..............................32mo, Paper   20
Romance on Four Wheels...................................   15
Second-Cousin Sarah. Illustrated........................   50
Stern Necessity..   40
The Barmaid at Battleton.................32mo, Paper   15
The Black Speck..........................32mo, Paper   10
The Romance of a Back Street.............32mo, Paper   15
True to Herself..   50
THACKERAY'S (W. M.) Denis Duval. Illustrated.............   25
Henry Esmond and Lovel the Widower. 12 Illustrations......   60
Henry Esmond...   50

4to, Paper   15

Lovel the Widower..   20
Pendennis.   179 Illustrations...........................   75
The Adventures of Philip.   64 Illustrations.................   60
The Great Hoggarty Diamond..............................   20
The Newcomes.   162 Illustrations.......................   90
The Virginians.   150 Illustrations.....................   90
Vanity Fair. 32 Illustrations..........................   80
THACKERAY'S Works: Household Edition........12mo, per vol. 1 25
Novels: Vanity Fair. — Pendennis. — The Newcomes. — The
Virginians.—Philip.—Esmond, and Lovel the Widower. 6
vols. Illustrated.
Miscellaneous : Barry Lyndon, Hoggarty Diamond, &c.—Paris
and Irish Sketch Books, &c.—Book of Snobs, Sketches, &c.—
Four Georges, English Humorists, Roundabout Papers, &c.
—Catharine, &c. 5 vols. Illustrated.

PRICE

TROLLOPE'S (Anthony) The Bertrams...........................12mo $1 50

                                                           4to, Paper   15

    The Claverings.   Illustrated   50

                                                             Cloth 1 00

    The Duke's Children............................4to, Paper   20

    The Eustace Diamonds.   Illustrated................................   80

                                                               Cloth 1 30

    The Golden Lion of Granpere.   Illustrated.....................   40

                                                                  Cloth   90

    The Lady of Launay.......................32mo, Paper   20

    The Last Chronicle of Barset.   Illustrated......................   90

                                                               Cloth 1 40

    The Prime Minister   60

    The Small House at Allington.   Illustrated......................   75

                                                               Cloth 1 25

    The Three Clerks.........................12mo 1 50

    The Vicar of Bullhampton.   Illustrated..........................   80

                                                               Cloth 1 30

    The Warden and Barchester Towers.   In one volume..........   60

    The Way we Live Now.   Illustrated..............................   90

                                                               Cloth 1 40

    Thompson Hall.   Illustrated..........................32mo, Paper   20

TWO Tales of Married Life..   30

WALLACE'S (Lew) Ben-Hur..........................16mo, Cloth 1 50

WAVERLEY NOVELS:

      THISTLE EDITION: 48 Vols., Green Cloth, with 2000 Illustrations, $1 00 per vol. ; Half Morocco, Gilt Tops, $1 50 per vol. ; Half Morocco, Extra, $2 25 per vol.

      HOLYROOD EDITION: 48 Vols., Brown Cloth, with 2000 Illustrations, 75 cents per vol.; Half Morocco, Gilt Tops, $1 50 per vol.; Half Morocco, Extra, $2 25 per vol.

      POPULAR EDITION: 24 Vols. (two vols. in one), Green Cloth, with 2000 Illustrations, $1 25 per vol.; Half Morocco, $2 25 per vol.; Half Morocco, Extra, $3 00 per vol.

      Waverley; Guy Mannering; The Antiquary; Rob Roy; Old Mortality; The Heart of Mid-Lothian; A Legend of Montrose; The Bride of Lammermoor; The Black Dwarf; Ivanhoe; The Monastery; The Abbot; Kenilworth; The Pirate; The Fortunes of Nigel; Peveril of the Peak; Quentin Durward; St. Ronan's Well; Redgauntlet; The Betrothed; The Talisman; Woodstock; Chronicles of the Canongate, The Highland Widow, &c.; The Fair Maid of Perth; Anne of Geierstein; Count Robert of Paris; Castle Dangerous; The Surgeon's Daughter; Glossary.

☞ HARPER & BROTHERS *will send any of the above works by mail, postage prepaid, to any part of the United States, on receipt of the price.*